AUTHOR'S NOTE

When I started writing the Willow Park series four years ago, it felt like I was doing something risky. I wanted to write about characters whose religious faith was important to them, but I also wanted to write for a mainstream romance audience (which has been the readership of all my books). I was surprised and gratified by the positive reception Willow Park received, although certainly there was too much religion in them for some readers and too little for others. I continue to be interested and emotionally invested in seeing religious faith (of all varieties) be explored more frequently in contemporary romance. This book, like the Willow Park books, tells the story of characters for whom faith commitments are very important, and so the plot and themes reflect that. I tried very hard to make it engaging and accessible for any reader of romance and for the spiritual themes not to alienate readers. Whether I succeeded at this challenge has yet to be decided and is likely open for debate, but as I said when I published *Married for Christmas*, I do believe it's worth the attempt.

ONE

"Why is that person riding a horse on the side of the road?"

John's question was sharp, skeptical, causing Betsy to jump in surprise. She'd thought he'd dozed off in the passenger seat as she drove, but he clearly wasn't asleep now.

She'd just pulled over into the oncoming traffic lane to steer clear of a woman on a black mare, walking peacefully down the road. She glanced into the rearview mirror to get another glimpse of the horse. "I guess she has somewhere to go."

"So she rides a horse on a busy road."

"Horses are big here. There are wild horses up in Corolla. You can't get there to see them without a four-wheel drive."

"That wasn't a wild horse."

"I know. I'm just saying. People like horses here."

John shook his head and muttered, "Silly."

Betsy had heard that curt word muttered countless times in the years she'd known John. It was his all-encompassing judgment on anything he found trivial, anything he saw as unproductive.

Usually she found it kind of funny. He often said it in half jest. He didn't seem to be joking this time though, and she didn't find it amusing. "I'm sure she enjoys it," she said lightly.

"So where exactly are we going?" John demanded.

"I told you," she said quietly, trying to keep her eyes wide and her expression innocent. "It's a place on the Outer

Banks. We should be there in twenty or twenty-five minutes now."

"What place?"

John Davenport was the leader of a crisis response team with a Christian international relief organization. Betsy had worked for the organization for eight years, and she'd been part of John's team for four. He was her boss—which was one of the reasons her present mission was so awkward.

There were a lot of reasons. She'd been dreading it for weeks.

John was used to being in charge, being active, having people do as he said. He wasn't used to downtime or to being driven to places he didn't know.

"It's a place on the beach. Chuck and Curtis arranged it for you."

Chuck was John's boss, and Curtis was Chuck's boss. Betsy was prepared to use their authority to ensure that John followed the plans they'd made.

She'd rehearsed this conversation many times for the past several weeks, but at the moment, she couldn't remember what she'd practiced. Her heart was beating so loud she thought John might be able to hear it.

Both John and Betsy were on a month-long sabbatical—John having been forced into the required break with much argument. Betsy was going to spend time with her mother in Buxton, her hometown. John was going somewhere else.

"What place is it, Betsy? Something isn't feeling right about it."

"It is right."

"You said it was a resort."

"It is—of a kind."

"Of what kind?"

She sighed. She'd volunteered to break this news to him because she thought he'd take it better from her, but now she was starting to regret it. "It's a rest-and-retreat center." Might as well just say it outright. There wasn't much time left to delay since they weren't very far away. They'd reached the coast and were headed south along the Outer Banks. They'd be to their destination soon.

He was silent for a moment. "And everyone is going to be there?"

She cleared her throat. "N-no. Just you."

"What?" John tended to be a blunt man with a loud voice. His soft, hoarse tone was very uncharacteristic.

It caused Betsy's stomach to twist. "It's a really great place—right on the beach. You'll like it."

"I will not like it."

"You have no idea whether you'll like it or not. You have to give it a chance." Leave it to John to put the pieces together in a few seconds and know exactly what was happening and why it was happening. He'd always been the quickest thinker she'd ever known.

"I don't have to do anything. When you said they'd arranged a retreat, I assumed it would be for everyone. I'm not sick or damaged or psychologically troubled. I don't need a damn—"

"No one is saying you are. But Chuck and Curtis think—"

"This place is right near your hometown?"

"Yes. Fairly close. Several miles north."

"And you're saying this was Chuck and Curtis's idea?"

Betsy swallowed. Of course he would realize this particular retreat center had been her suggestion. "It was their *decision*," she said firmly. "It's a really nice place."

"Why does everyone suddenly think I've lost it?" He was scowling and staring ahead of them at the busy two-lane road lined with beach shops, fishing stores, and quirky restaurants. The road ran the length of the Outer Banks, a string of peninsulas and barrier islands on the coast of North Carolina. He looked bad-tempered, but Betsy knew it was more than that.

He was upset. He didn't want anyone to think he was weak or damaged. He'd always been that way. She was that way too—to a lesser extent—so she could understand how he felt.

"No one thinks you've lost it," she said, keeping her voice as calm as she could, although she was feeling upset now too. "This isn't a mental health facility, although there would be nothing wrong with that. It's a rest-and-retreat center, and that means exactly what it sounds like. You're tired. You won't admit it, but everyone knows it's true. You're on the edge of being burned out, and if you keep it up, you won't be able to do your work."

"I am not that—"

"Yes, you are. You've been snapping at people and picking arguments and working sixteen hours a day. We've worked crisis after crisis—every one of them horrifying and heartbreaking—and you didn't take the break two years ago that you were supposed to. Not to mention all the trauma with your brother you've had to deal with."

John's brother, Mark, had been a journalist working in the Middle East when he was taken hostage by a Syrian rebel group. He'd been held by the group for two years and had only been released eighteen months ago. Although his story had had a happy ending, and John had never revealed his feelings to

4

her, Betsy knew the fear and grief over the years had eaten him up.

"Mark's thing is over now," John muttered.

"I know. But that doesn't mean it didn't wear on you. You're exhausted, John. All of us can see it."

"That's why I took the sabbatical. I don't need to go to some place for counseling and coddling."

"No one is going to coddle you—or counsel you if you don't want it. You need rest. You only took the sabbatical because you were forced into it, and there's no way to ensure you'll actually get the rest you need."

"Damn it, Bets."

Betsy had been raised by an old-fashioned mother and had come to faith in a very conservative church. It wasn't until she was an adult that she'd met sincere Christians who talked like John and had wine with dinner and could talk about sex without blushing. But even John didn't use *damn* several times in one conversation very often, so she knew his mood was declining quickly.

He continued, "I don't want—"

"It doesn't matter what you want," she interrupted sharply, about to lose it herself. She'd known this discussion would be hard, but she hadn't expected it to be this bad. "It doesn't matter. This is straight from Chuck and Curtis. You're to spend two weeks at this place. Then you're to spend the next two weeks visiting your brother. If you don't do it, you're not coming back after the sabbatical."

John stared at her, his vivid blue eyes almost dazed—like he'd just suffered a crushing blow.

"I'm sorry," she said, her voice breaking slightly. "I know it sounds terrible, but we know you and we love you, and you've refused to take days off and vacations for too long. You have to really rest, or you're going to break. Just do this. Just *do* it. Please."

He didn't answer for a long time, and Betsy had to turn back to look at the road. She was close to tears now, her eyes and throat burning.

Then he finally asked gruffly, "So what is this place?"

She sighed in relief, realizing he'd accepted the inevitable.

John loved his work as much as she did—and he was driven in a way she'd never been. He wasn't prepared to give it all up just to be stubborn.

"It's called Balm in Gilead."

He groaned.

"Stop it. It's a great place. It's like a resort, and it's right on the beach."

"Am I going to be stuck in there with a bunch of spoiled, rich people?"

"No. I don't think so. It serves a lot of people in the ministry. There will probably be a lot of folks there like you."

"Am I going to have to sit through endless counseling sessions and group-share times?"

She chuckled at his dry words. "No. They do offer one-on-one counseling, but you don't have to do it if you don't want. And I don't think there are any group sessions you'll be required to attend."

"So what do I do?"

"You rest. You take it easy. You walk on the beach. You participate in some of the activities they offer—you can pick and choose which ones, although I think there's a minimum number required each week. You try to relax."

He sighed loudly. "Fine. I don't know why I can't just relax in Willow Park with my brother though."

"Because there will be no accountability there. There is here."

"So I'm going to have to rest even if it kills me."

She smiled, relieved that he was sounding more like himself. "Yes. Exactly."

"And you won't be far away?"

She felt a slight flush warm her cheeks at the implication of the words. "My mom's place is about ten miles away. I can come visit you if you want."

"You'll come every day?"

She blinked, trying to control the flush on her cheeks. She'd always been fair-skinned though, and there was no way to stop herself from blushing. "Sure. I'll come if you want."

"You better. If I'm going to be stuck there for two weeks, I'll need someone I know to complain to."

She let out a breath.

Of course that was why he wanted her to visit.

They worked together, so they knew each other well. He was her boss, and he relied on her a lot for the administrative tasks and communication. She was pretty sure that most of the time John considered her a friend.

He'd never looked at her as anything else, and she knew he never would.

She'd never been the kind of woman men looked at romantically anyway.

~

The Balm in Gideon Center for Rest was located about halfway down the Outer Banks. It consisted of thirty acres of property and included a private beach. The main building was three stories and sided in weathered cedar, and the front lawns and side garden were obviously well tended because the grass was richly green and as smooth as velvet.

Betsy had often gone by the property when she was a kid and it had been an exclusive hotel resort—one of the nicest on the Outer Banks—and she'd daydreamed about being rich enough to stay there. Now nearly everyone rented the vacation houses that lined the coast, so the hotel had closed ten years ago.

Eight years ago, Cecily Evans had opened this retreat center. Betsy felt strange, pulling onto the long driveway. For a minute she felt like a little girl again.

A little girl who didn't belong here at all.

Then John demanded, "How much does this place cost?"

"It doesn't matter. Chuck and Curtis are taking care of it."

"I don't want them to be wasting a lot of money on me that could be used—"

"We got a discount."

John's blue eyes were questioning, always intelligent. "How did we finagle a discount?"

"I... I know Cecily, who runs the place. I kind of know her. We went to the same school, although she was several years older than me. She gave us a discount."

"You didn't make me into some kind of pity case, did you?"

"No, no. Of course not. I just touched base with her and explained what we needed. She offered the discount. I think she does that a lot with people in ministry. She must make enough money charging rich folks high prices so she can afford to help. Like I said, I know her. She was trying to be nice."

John nodded and reached into the back seat to grab the beat-up leather saddlebag he used as a briefcase.

She felt a little flutter of nerves when she saw the bag and knew his laptop was inside, but she decided not to broach the topic quite yet.

They needed to get in the door first.

She was opening the trunk for John to grab his suitcase when they became aware of a presence behind them.

Turning to look, her eyes widened when she saw a big, dark-haired, glowering man with an untrimmed beard. He wore faded jeans and a T-shirt of a surprisingly bright melon color. He didn't say a word. Just took the suitcase out of John's hand and made a wordless gesture toward the front door.

He must work here, although this hadn't been much of a greeting or a welcome.

John rolled his eyes slightly and started toward the front door.

Betsy's stomach twisted again. This wasn't an auspicious beginning.

John was already in a bad mood.

They walked up the steps to a wide deck on the main floor of the building, and John opened one of the double doors of what was clearly the main entrance.

The lobby was big and airy with a beautifully tiled floor and a wall of windows in the back, looking out onto the patio and pool.

The bearded man had followed them and gave a kind of grunt as he nodded toward the elevators.

"We appreciate your hospitality," John said, a dry edge of irony in his tone that was impossible to mistake.

"Please don't mind Zeke," a polished female voice came from the other side of them.

Betsy turned her head to see Cecily Evans stepping out of what looked to be an office. She looked exactly as she had always looked—tall, slim, beautiful, and perfect with ash brown hair pulled into a low bun, subtle makeup, heels, and small glasses that gave her an almost prim look.

She smiled at both of them graciously. "Zeke has his own way about him, and that way is not charming. But he's worked here since we opened, and he can help you with anything you need. Just try to overlook his bearlike qualities."

Zeke was standing next to the elevators—not very far away—so he must have heard her words. But obviously they didn't surprise or offend him since he didn't even turn his head to look in their direction.

"I'm Cecily," she added with another smile, extending a hand, complete with perfect french manicure, to John. "You must be John Davenport."

His face relaxed slightly, and Betsy could tell he liked Cecily a lot more than Zeke. "Yeah. It's nice to meet you."

"Your room is on the third floor." She handed him a key and a folder in which was obviously information about the center. "Zeke will show you. I'll let you get settled, but when you feel like it, come on down and I'll show you around."

Betsy was relieved Cecily wasn't going to join them on the trip up to the room, mostly because she didn't want the other woman around when John found out a few details of his stay here.

They ascended the elevator with a silent, unsmiling Zeke—Betsy noticed his eyes were as blue as John's—and they followed him down a hallway.

Betsy gasped in pleasure as they walked into a big, sunny room. It was decorated in an attractive, simple way in shades of green and beige, but the furniture was of good quality and the artwork was original. There was a glass door that led out onto a balcony large enough to fit a chaise and two chairs.

"This is amazing," she said.

"This doesn't look like a discount room to me," John said. He clearly thought it was nice too.

"We're not full," Zeke grunted, parking the luggage next to the bed. Then he just walked out the door.

"Nice," John muttered, clearly annoyed by the other man.

"Don't worry about him," Betsy said, hoping the pleasantness of the room would make up for his reluctance to be here. "Isn't this a great room?"

"Yeah. It's something."

"Please, John," she said softly. "You've got to stay here. Can't you try to make the best of it?"

She could see a brief struggle on his face until his features finally smoothed out. "Okay. Fine."

The tension in her chest relaxed slightly. "It's really a nice place, and I don't think you'll find it too annoying. The information is probably in that folder, but basically you can do what you want, as long as you participate in five physical activities a week and five creative activities a week."

He would have no trouble with the physical activities—he'd always stayed in great shape—but she wasn't surprised by the way his brows arched. "Creative?"

"It won't be that bad. Most of the time, you can do what you want."

He took a deep breath and let it out. Then jerked when the door to the room swung open again and Zeke made another appearance.

He held out his hand. "Electronics."

John stared at the other man. "What?"

"He wants your electronic devices," Betsy said, knowing the time had finally come. "They're not allowed here."

John's mouth dropped open slightly. "They're not allowed?"

"No. Sorry. That's part of the way you get rest. No phones or tablets or… or…"

"I can't have my laptop?"

Betsy shook her head.

"Forget it."

"John—"

"That's ridiculous. What will I do when people need to reach me?"

"You set up an away message on your email, didn't you?"

"Sure. Of course. But I was still planning to check in sometimes. What if there's an emergency?"

"We've got people covering for emergencies. Sabbatical means a real break."

"And I really can't have my phone?"

She shook her head. "You can use the landline here if you need to call out, but it can't be anything work related. I'm sorry. I know it's hard, but it really works to take a break from it. You can leave a voice message to deal with calls, or I can cover them for you if you want."

He wasn't convinced. He was still planning to object.

She added, "John, it's the rule here. You have to do it."

He let out a breath, more of a groan. "Damn it, Bets. How could you do this to me?"

She jerked slightly, feeling like she'd been slapped, although she knew she couldn't take it personally.

This had been dumped on John without warning. He'd had no time to prepare himself. She, Chuck, and Curtis had decided it was better to do it this way so he wouldn't be able to worm his way out of it, but there were consequences to their decision.

One of the consequences was that John was going to resent her for it.

"I'm sorry," she said, pleased when her voice sounded mostly natural. "But you don't have a choice in this."

He was frowning as he dug into his saddlebag, pulled out his laptop, and handed it to Zeke. He took his phone from his pocket and handed it to Betsy.

She saw his hand on another device he'd pulled out of his bag.

"He doesn't have to give up his Kindle, does he? It's the only way he reads books."

When Zeke studied the e-reader suspiciously, Betsy added, "It doesn't have web browsing capabilities. It's just for reading."

Zeke gave a brief nod, and Betsy let out a breath of relief.

When Zeke left the room, John slumped into a chair. "I'm going to hate this."

"Give it a chance. Maybe you won't."

"I'm not the kind of person who takes it easy."

"I know. That's why you ended up here."

He gave her a little scowl, but there wasn't much animosity in it.

He wasn't happy, but he didn't seem to hate her.

That was something.

~

An hour later, Betsy had left John and driven the fifteen minutes to her mother's house.

Her mother had lived here most of her life, long before it had become a popular tourist destination. Betsy had never known her father since her mother had not been married when she got pregnant and her father had just taken off. Betsy had tried to convince her mother to move to a nicer and more convenient place, but her mother had refused to leave the little house Betsy had been raised in, on the outskirts of Buxton, one of the little towns that dotted the Outer Banks.

The neat yard, old house, and cheerful welcome mat were all exactly as she remembered. As was the hug her mother gave her and the tea she made.

They sat at the kitchen table, drinking the tea as Betsy told her mother about the plan for John and his reaction.

"I don't blame him for being annoyed," Betsy added. "We really did spring it on him."

"But it sounds like it's for the best. The break will be good for him."

"Yeah." Betsy felt a little glum, despite her pleasure at seeing her mother again. She didn't see her mother nearly as much as she wanted because her job required so much travel.

"It will be good for you too," her mother added as if she'd read some of her thoughts. "Maybe it will be a good time for you to reevaluate."

"What does that mean?"

Her mother gave an innocent shrug. "Nothing bad. Just that it might be a good time to think through what you want for the future."

"Mom, we've talked about this. I love my job. I want to keep doing it."

"I know you do, honey. And I've always supported you. But you've just turned thirty. And you travel all the time, you haven't put down any roots, and you don't even have a home except that tiny studio apartment in Charlotte. There's almost no chance of you finding a man to marry and settle down with given the life you lead. Are you saying you don't want that?"

"Sure, I'd like to get married, but it just hasn't happened yet. Right now my job is the priority. I'm telling you, I'm perfectly happy."

She meant it. She absolutely meant it. She tried not to lie to her mother.

"I believe you. But maybe you can think about how you'll feel when John finds a woman he wants to marry. Would things still be the same then? Would you still be perfectly happy?"

Betsy swallowed hard, strangely stunned by the question.

She wanted to automatically defend herself, prove her mother wrong, but she couldn't do it.

The truth was nothing would be the same if John was married.

They'd always been more like partners than boss and team member. His companionship was one of the things she loved about her life, along with the community of the rest of the team. She never felt lonely because she was always surrounded by people she knew and loved.

But it wouldn't be the same if John was married.

It wouldn't be the same at all.

"I'm not nursing some kind of hopeless crush on him," she said at last. "I've never been that silly."

She'd realized soon after meeting him that John would never look at her romantically. He was incredibly attractive and charismatic in a loud, opinionated way. Women were always looking at him longingly. She could see it even if he appeared oblivious to it.

Betsy had dated occasionally, but the only guys who asked her out were the needy sort—not the kind she was interested in. There was nothing in her capable of attracting a guy like John. Besides, he was utterly consumed by his work, to the exclusion of anything else in his life.

"I know you've never really let yourself think in that direction. But the heart doesn't always do what it's told. And for a long time, you two have been acting like a couple."

"We have not—"

"I'm not saying anything inappropriate has happened between you. I'm just saying that you work together so closely that you've relied on each other for emotional support. Like a couple. And I can't help but worry about how you'll feel when—five or ten years from now—John finally decides to settle down and marry. He'll be able to do that. He's a man. He'll be able to find someone easily enough, no matter how old he is. But you might be over forty by then. What if you want to have children? What if it's too late for you to have your chance?"

Betsy was shaking slightly now, and she raised a hand to cover her eyes. She was usually a composed, matter-of-fact person—in fact, she was known for it—but at the moment she felt like crying.

Her mother was right.

She was perfectly happy in her job right now, but she did have other things she wanted in life.

Marriage and family were two of them.

She wasn't likely to ever find that if she continued living the way she was.

"I don't want to give up my work."

"I don't want you to give it up either. But maybe you can find a different work situation—one that will allow you to have a full life."

"I... I don't know."

Her mother nodded and reached out to cover one of her hands on the table. "Just think about it, dear. You don't have to figure it out right now. You have a month off. You need the break as much as John does. Maybe by the end of it, you'll have a clearer idea of what you want."

This morning, Betsy would never have believed that she'd be questioning her job in any way.

But she was now.

It was heartbreaking to consider leaving a position she loved so much, but most people didn't last very long in the job she did. It was hard on people psychologically, and it was hard in terms of lifestyle. Maybe it had always only been temporary for her too.

She loved working with John, but it had been clear from the beginning that he couldn't offer her everything she wanted.

TWO

John woke up feeling stupid.

He'd been genuinely annoyed the day before, and he was convinced most people would have been as well—after being manipulated the way he'd been in being brought here by Betsy and his supervisors.

But he woke up when sunlight started to stream in from the edges of the curtains, and the first feeling he was aware of was embarrassment.

He thought of himself as a competent and independent person. People usually listened when he spoke and looked to him for answers.

He wasn't the kind of person that others needed to plot about behind his back. He wasn't weak and helpless.

But he couldn't help but feel that way as he hauled himself out of bed.

He hadn't slept well.

He traveled so much that he wasn't usually afflicted with jet lag, but he normally woke up a few times during the night to check his phone. He'd woken up four times last night, but when he'd reached for the nightstand, he'd had no phone to check.

The lack of it left him feeling naked, ineffectual.

He didn't like it.

Betsy had been right when she'd said that he needed to suck it up and get through this though. He couldn't lose his job. It was the way he contributed to the world. He would be nothing without it. So he forced himself into the shower and into clothes before he made his way downstairs.

Meals were served in the large dining room, and he was pleased to see that seating options included both communal tables and individual ones.

He got his food from a self-serve buffet and went to a small table by the window instead of joining the few others already up and seated at one of the large tables.

He didn't want to talk to strangers this morning. He wasn't fit company.

He wasn't a bit hungry today. In fact, his stomach was churning uncomfortably.

His team's last job had been in Sudan, trying to bring relief to the victims of a widespread famine that had decimated large communities. The faces of the people he'd interacted with—gaunt men and women, dying children—still haunted him.

There was one boy named Jamal—about six years old. He'd liked to talk to John about baseball and cars. He'd been so sick when John had left.

Hopefully, he was responding to the medical treatment they'd provided.

That famine was horrifying, and so few people in the world were even talking about it.

No matter how little he felt like eating, John wasn't about to leave food uneaten on his plate.

He said a silent grace, asking God to change his attitude and thanking him for the food, but John didn't feel any better afterward.

In fact, he felt more guilty, less hungry.

He swallowed down half a cup of coffee before he started to eat.

The food was surprisingly good—he'd expected the typical tasteless eggs and rubbery bacon found on most breakfast buffets—but he didn't really enjoy it. As he kept putting food into his mouth, he looked out the window. His seat looked out onto the far end of the patio. The ocean wasn't visible from the first floor because the sand dunes were too high, but the view of the pool, with the dunes beyond and a crisp blue sky above, was still quite pleasant.

Instead of admiring it, John focused on a seagull pecking at what looked like an old french fry.

The bird was very small for a gull, and the fry must have been ancient. It was evidently as hard as a rock because the bird kept pecking and pecking but made very little progress.

The view completely captivated him—going on for more than ten minutes—and when he was finished eating, the bird still hadn't managed to get more than a few little crumbs.

"Would you like some more coffee?" a female voice came from above him.

He responded with an automatic yes before he turned his head to see the server was in fact Cecily Evans, the owner and manager.

She was dressed in another skirt and silk blouse with her hair pulled back just like it had been the day before. He wasn't sure why she dressed up so much in a beach setting like this, but maybe she found the professional appearance helped her maintain authority.

It could be difficult for attractive women to be in charge. He'd seen it happen in various professional settings more than once.

"Thanks," he said, realizing she was waiting for him to speak.

She seemed nice enough and competent, but John had to stifle a groan when she set the coffee pot down on the table and sat in the chair across from him.

He didn't really feel like being friendly this morning.

It wasn't Cecily's fault he was in a bad mood though, so he managed to smile. "Am I supposed to be socializing?" he asked, nodding toward the large table where more people had gathered. There were about twelve of them now.

Her eyes widened behind her glasses. "No. Of course not. There's never any pressure to socialize here."

"Really?"

"Really. A lot of my guests here are in business and in ministry—and they're forced every day to interact with people. Doing so is part of their job. This place is about rest, and one of the ways people in your position can find rest is by being freed of the pressure of socializing. Some people make friends here, and so they enjoy talking to others. But for others it's a luxury to be able to simply sit in silence."

John had never thought about that before, but he was glad he wouldn't be given any guilt-trips about not making friends.

He nodded by way of response.

Cecily was watching him with intelligent eyes. "There's no pressure here. As long as you check off your weekly activities, you can do whatever you like with the rest of your time."

"Okay. Thanks." He still felt rather stupid—like he wasn't the kind of person who should be at a place that had a weekly checklist of activities. But at least it wouldn't be as bad as he'd feared.

"I believe they're looking for a fourth for tennis this morning," Cecily said, nodding toward the large table. "If you like to play."

"I don't mind it, but I'd rather run if that's okay."

"Of course."

John frowned. "If they really need someone—"

"No, no. What did I just say? There's no pressure. I'm sure they'll find their fourth when more people come down for breakfast. You can run on the beach, of course, or if you prefer pavement, it's safe to run along the main road. In the mornings particularly, when there's less traffic."

"I'll run on the beach. I don't mind the sand."

Cecily inclined her head to acknowledge his words but didn't say anything else immediately.

John sipped his coffee and looked back down at the bird by the window, who was still futilely pecking out the stale fry.

"How long have you known Betsy?" Cecily asked, still sounding friendly and conversational.

"I don't know. Like eight years or something? Since she started working for my organization. She's been part of my team now for four years. She said you're from her hometown?"

"Yes. We went to the same school, although she's quite a bit younger than I am. Everyone in town is very proud of the work she does. Her mother talks about her all the time."

"Good," John murmured over the rim of his coffee cup. "Bets is pretty great."

Cecily smiled. "I remember one year I came home on a college break, and she was in junior high, and she'd organized a food drive for a homeless shelter. You wouldn't believe how organized and enthusiastic she was, even as a kid. She ended up with a whole truckload of food for the shelter—more than they'd ever been given before."

John couldn't help but chuckle. "That sounds like her. She takes care of everything for our team. I couldn't function without her."

He felt another stab of guilt for the way he'd snapped at Betsy yesterday. She'd been trying to take care of things—take care of him—the way she always did. She didn't deserve that attitude from him.

"I can imagine." Cecily cleared her throat and started to stand up. "Hopefully, she'll be able to visit you some while you're here."

"She said she would."

John sure as hell hoped she would. She'd promised to come every day.

"I can catch up with her sometime then. I hope you have a great day." With another professional smile, Cecily took her coffee pot and moved on to the large table.

John finished his coffee, thinking about what Betsy must have been like as a child. When he finished, he walked back over to the buffet and picked up a biscuit as he left the room.

He went outside, walking across the patio to look out over the walkway across the dunes that led to the ocean.

On his way there, he discreetly crumbled up the biscuit and scattered the pieces near the stale french fry so the hungry seagull could have a treat.

~

John ran for almost two hours that morning until he was drenched with sweat and absolutely exhausted. Then he showered again and went down to the large deck on the second floor with views of the ocean.

He stretched out on a chaise with a bottle of water and his Kindle, and he started a new book by a theologian he admired on a biblical approach to ministry.

His mind was racing with ideas as he read—about possible ways to implement some of these principals on his team and in the larger organization.

He was so absorbed in the book that he didn't even notice when someone sat down on the chaise beside him.

When he finally became aware of the presence, he looked up with a frown. He didn't like people hovering around him.

He blinked in surprise to discover it was Betsy.

She looked fresh, pretty, and smiling, and he couldn't help but smile back.

"Hi," she said. "That must be a good book."

"It is," he said.

He wasn't sure why he thought she looked so pretty this morning. Her light brown hair was pulled back in its normal ponytail, and her clear skin and even features were free of makeup. She wore jeans, a white T-shirt, and sandals, which was a normal outfit for her.

Maybe it was just because he was used to seeing her all the time, and he hadn't seen her in twenty hours.

Since he found the feeling disturbing, he immediately switched gears to something more comfortable and familiar. "Did I get any email?" he asked.

Her smile faded slightly. "A couple. Nothing important."

"Who were they from?"

"It doesn't matter. I forwarded them on to Rick. He'll take care of them."

John stifled the frustration over not having control of his own email account. "Calls?"

"Just Mark. I talked to him for a bit."

"He knew about me coming here?" He didn't like the idea that his brother—who had been through so much more than John ever would—knew he was being coddled this way.

"Yes. I ran it by him before we arranged everything. He thought it was a good idea."

This made John scowl slightly, but he was determined to be less grumpy today, so he didn't speak his thoughts.

"He said he'd call you later," Betsy added.

"How is he going to reach me?"

"The landline here. You're allowed to talk to your family."

He managed not to grumble about how that was all he was allowed to do.

They sat in silence for a minute. Then Betsy reached over to take his e-reader from his hand and looked down at the screen. That was just like her. No standing on ceremony or artifice. If she wanted to do something, she just did it.

She started to frown as she peered down at his Kindle. "Why are you reading this?"

"Because I want to."

"But it's a work book."

"I don't care. This is the kind of thing I read." His happy feelings at her appearance were starting to dim.

"You're supposed to be on a break. Why don't you try reading a novel or two?"

"I don't like novels. I like nonfiction."

"You like work books."

"Whatever you want to call it, this is what I read."

She looked bad-tempered now too. "If all you're going to read are things about work, then I'm going to take your Kindle with me."

"You're not going to do anything of the kind. I'm not a child, you know."

"I never said you're a child." Her cheeks were slightly flushed, and her eyes were flashing. She looked prettier than ever. "But you're supposed to be resting."

"I can rest and also read the kind of books I want to read. You can force me to be here, but you can't force me to change who I am."

"No one is trying to change who you are. You're being ridiculous."

"*I'm* being ridiculous? You're the one whose saying there's something wrong with what I read."

"I'm not saying something is wrong with the book. I'm saying that it's work focused, when you're supposed to be thinking about something else."

He and Betsy argued occasionally. Things always came up with their jobs that they disagreed on. The arguments were rarely heated, and they always quickly blew over. John wasn't sure why he was feeling so resentful right now—over such a little thing. But he heard himself snapping, "It's not your place to tell me what I'm supposed to be doing. You're not my boss or my girlfriend."

He'd gone too far. He knew he'd gone too far. He knew it as soon as the words had come out of his mouth, even before he saw Betsy jerk slightly, like he'd slapped her.

Betsy was important to him. She didn't just work for him. It was utterly wrong to imply she was nothing to him but a team member.

"Sorry," he muttered.

She gave her head a little shake and then gave him a smile that didn't reach her eyes. "It's fine. I shouldn't have pushed."

He was silently cursing himself and searching his mind for some way to make it better. "It was me. It wasn't you."

She smiled again, but this one was just as fake as the one before.

He'd hurt her. She was trying not to let it show, but he could see it so clearly.

"It's fine," she said, her voice mostly natural. He wasn't fooled for a minute though. "I know it's hard for you to be here, and I'm sorry that we had to trick you into it. I can't stay very long today anyway. I just wanted to drop by and say hi and give you this." She handed him a brown paper shopping bag.

"What is it?"

"Just a few things." She stood up and was still holding on to that terrible, fake smile, the one that was killing him to see. "I can drop by tomorrow if you want."

His throat was hurting, and his heart was racing, and he couldn't think of a single thing to say to make this better. "That would be great. Thanks."

She nodded and smiled and kept nodding and smiling until she finally turned around and walked away.

John stared after her, almost shaking with how stupid he had been.

Then he idly opened the bag to look down into it.

Inside were a few paperback books—novels, he immediately noticed—a container of what looked like homemade brownies, a pack of playing cards, and pair of binoculars.

She'd put together some little things that he might be able to use while he was here. Small things but thoughtful, generous, sweet.

"Damn it," he muttered, slipping his Kindle into the bag and standing up. He ran back into the building, down the stairs, and through the lobby.

He caught up with Betsy as she was walking down the front steps to the parking area.

"Bets!" he called. "Betsy, wait!"

She stopped and turned around, staring at him in surprise.

"I'm sorry," he said breathlessly, pulling to a stop right in front of her. "I'm really sorry."

"You already said that. I understand. I really do. It's no big deal."

"It is a big deal. I should never have treated you like that. You're really… really important to me. And thank you for the stuff."

She nodded and dropped her eyes.

He pulled his brows together and tilted up her chin so he could see her face. He didn't want her to still be upset. He didn't want her to be pretending to be fine with things.

He wanted her to like him again.

He froze for a moment when he saw a single tear sliding down her cheek.

She swiped it away quickly, clearly not wanting him to see it.

He had seen it though. She wasn't a woman who cried much or easily.

"Oh damn, Bets," he murmured. "I'm so sorry."

"You don't have to say it again." She'd squared her shoulders and was meeting his eyes now. "It's not a big deal. Really."

"But you're—"

"I'm not crying," she insisted, despite the evidence to the contrary. "I don't know what's wrong with me. I think it's being home, relaxing. I'm just kind of… letting down. I'm more tired than I realized. It's really nothing. I didn't mean to make you feel bad."

"I deserve to feel bad. You've been great to me. I've been the ass."

She gave a little shrug, but her smile now was real. Slightly wobbly, but real.

He exhaled in relief. "I'm really sorry."

"Please don't say it again."

"Do you really have to go so soon?"

"I…" She dropped her eyes and then raised them again. "I should have lunch with my mother."

"How is she doing?"

"She's pretty good. Her knees are really bothering her, but otherwise she's healthy. She's staying just as busy as always."

"Give her my best."

"I will."

"Thanks for the stuff."

"You're welcome. You don't have to read the books if you don't want."

"I'll give them a try."

She smiled at him, and he knew he'd said the right thing for once.

"You'll come tomorrow?" He was surprised that his voice sounded so urgent, as if it was the most important thing in the world that she return the next day.

"Yes. I'll come."

"Maybe you can stay longer."

She nodded. "Yes. Yes, I'm sure I can."

"Good."

They stared at each other in silence for a moment. Then she gave herself a little shake and turned away. "Bye."

"Bye, Betsy."

He stood and watched as she walked to her car. His eyes couldn't help but dip down to admire the rounded curve of her butt in her jeans. She wasn't built like a model. She wasn't very tall, and she had all kinds of tantalizing curves.

He hadn't been oblivious to this fact over the years, although he'd made sure to never let himself dwell on it.

He shouldn't be dwelling on it now.

He shouldn't. At all.

And he definitely shouldn't be letting his body find hers so interesting.

He'd been a failure in every way today.

He'd have to do better tomorrow.

~

John was reading that evening when there was a knock on his door.

He jerked in surprise and was even more surprised when he opened the door and was confronted with Zeke's unsmiling face.

"Phone call," the man muttered.

John raised his eyebrows. Betsy had mentioned that Mark might try to call him here, and it was evidently an acceptable arrangement according to the center's rules. But Zeke was scowling as if it was John's fault he'd had to walk up the stairs to make the announcement.

"Where can I take the call?" John asked a little coolly.

"Sitting room on the second floor." With that, Zeke turned around and walked away.

John rolled his eyes and resisted the temptation to make a rude comment to the other man's back.

He went downstairs to the private sitting room—a small, comfortable space with expansive views out onto the ocean—and he closed the door before picking up the extension to the landline.

"Hello? This is John."

"I'm hanging up now," a pleasant female voice said. It wasn't Cecily, so it must have been another member of the staff.

After the click, Mark said, "Hey. How are you doing?"

John felt a strangely intense wave of relief at hearing his brother's familiar voice. "Hey. I'm fine. Thanks for calling."

"I gather phone calls are a big event there, without cell phones."

"Seems like it." John shook his head at the empty room. "It's crazy they don't allow them."

"Sounds like there's good reason for it. Phones can really add to stress."

"If you say so."

Mark paused for a moment. "I guess you're still just as cranky as Betsy said you were."

John let out a breath and felt momentarily embarrassed. Maybe he really was being unreasonable lately. All his annoyance felt rational and supportable, but he supposed it always did when you were in the instance of it. He wasn't by nature a people pleaser, but he also didn't want everyone to hate being around him. "Sorry."

"It's fine. I know it must have been a shock to have this sprung on you."

"And yet everyone seems to think it was the right thing to do."

"Are you telling me you wouldn't have tried to get out of it, if you'd known it was coming?"

Of course he would have tried to get out of it. That much was obvious.

"Anyway, I didn't mean to sound cranky. I'm glad you called."

"I'm sorry I couldn't be out there when you arrived."

"There's no reason why you need to be. How have you been doing?"

Mark must have known from the change in John's tone that was he was asking more than just the normal polite question. He really wanted to know. "I've been doing good. Really good."

Eighteen months ago, when Mark had returned from the Middle East after being held hostage, he'd been a broken man, physically and emotionally. His healing hadn't been an easy thing, but even from halfway around the world, John could tell that every month he was getting stronger, happier.

"Are you still going to counseling?" John asked.

"Yeah, but just once a month now. I actually am doing better. It's a miracle, really."

"Well, you're really tough. That helps too."

"If you say so."

"You are. I don't know how many guys could have gotten through all that the way you did."

Mark cleared his throat. "Thanks," he muttered.

John didn't dwell since he knew it was making his brother uncomfortable. "How's Sophie?"

"She's great. Amazing as always."

"And things are going well between the two of you?"

"Yes. Really good. You don't have to check every time, you know. Things were touch and go with her at first, but we're better now. We really are."

"I'm glad. She's a keeper."

"You think I don't know that?"

"I don't know of any other woman who'd be willing to put up with you."

"Thanks a lot," Mark replied dryly. "At least there's one in the world—which is more than I can say of you."

John couldn't help but chuckle. "Probably better that way."

There was a strange silence on the line, as if Mark was trying to hold himself back from saying something. Normally, John would push to find out what he was thinking, but he was just as happy not to hear it at the moment.

"So nothing interesting is happening there?" John asked.

"Not really. Work is good. Church is good. Sophie and I had a huge fight about coffee this morning, so that was something, I guess."

"About coffee?" John said with a laugh. "What was that about?"

"I like my coffee a lot stronger than her—like reasonable people do. I don't know how she drinks such weak stuff. She calls it normal coffee, but it's weak-ass and barely drinkable. She used to be fine with the strong stuff—when we first got married and after I got back. But then she just announced she's never really liked it. Anyway, we tried to compromise for a while, but neither one of us liked the middle-ground coffee. So then we came up with a plan."

John was smiling as he listened to this story. "I can't wait to hear this."

"We would take turns. Alternating days. One day I'd make good coffee, and the next day she'd make her weak-ass stuff. And so on."

"And that didn't work?"

"She started getting up at five thirty to make her own coffee, even on my days. Then she'd pour the rest out and pretend she hadn't done anything. So I started getting up at five on her days to do the same thing. I mean, what else could I do?"

John was laughing out loud now. "Sounds reasonable. She caught you, didn't she?"

"Yes! And she got all outraged, like she hadn't been doing the same thing. She said she'd get up at four thirty from now on."

"Can't you just make two different pots of coffee?"

"Don't try to bring rationality into a perfectly good marital spat. It's the principle of the thing. Obviously."

John couldn't stop laughing. "Obviously." He stared out the big windows, momentarily taken off guard by how beautiful the ocean was with the moonlight barely glinting off the waves. "For Christmas, I'll get you all one of the one-cup brewers. That would solve your whole problem."

"Where would be the fun in that?" Mark's tone changed as he continued, "So how are things there? Are you having a good time?"

"I wouldn't exactly say that. I don't care for downtime like this."

"That's because you've never let yourself enjoy it. If you give it a try, I bet you'll have a good time."

"If you say so."

"I do say so," Mark said, ignoring John's sardonic tone. "You need to give it a try."

"I will."

"You were always like that."

"Always like what?"

"Remember when you were working on that car when you were twelve or thirteen?"

"Sure, I remember." He'd saved up his money and bought an ancient clunker that a neighbor had been going to send to the junkyard. He'd been convinced he could get it into working order again, and he'd worked for months after school to fix it up.

"You spent weeks on the transmission and couldn't get the thing working."

"Don't remind me. That damn thing drove me crazy."

"So finally Dad fixed it for you one night without telling you, and when you discovered it, you had a meltdown."

"It wasn't that bad."

"Not that bad? You were screaming your head off, and you took the whole thing apart again and spread out every little piece across the grass in the yard, just out of spite."

John was chuckling again at the memory. "I had my reasons. Like you said about the coffee, it was the principle of the thing."

"Dad was trying to help you, and you blew your top."

Suddenly realizing the purpose of this trip down memory lane, John grew still. After a moment, he said, "This little story had a moral, didn't it?"

"Not a moral. Just a point. You give help to anyone who asks for it. I can't even begin to count the number of stray animals you picked up when we were kids or all the bullied kids you stood up for. Anyone can see you've devoted your whole life to helping the people who need it the most. But you've never been able to accept help yourself. You think you have to work to earn it."

"I don't really."

"You do really. You think I don't know you? You need a break right now. Everyone who knows and loves you agrees on this. So just take it. Make the best of it. Okay?"

John fought back his instinctive resistance since he knew at heart that Mark was right. "Okay," he mumbled at last. "Okay. I'm trying, all right."

"Don't try. Just rest."

"Easier said than done."

"Yeah. I know. But those are all the words of wisdom I've got for you tonight."

They hung up a few minutes later, and John was surprised by how much better he felt as he returned to his room.

He thought a lot about how stupid and selfish he'd been as a child, throwing a fit when his father had tried to help.

His father—and his mother—had both died a few years later. John would give anything to have his dad to help him work on a car again.

THREE

Betsy woke up early, her mind whirling with thoughts and concerns and the restlessness she always felt when she was away from work, away from the field.

Deciding she needed to get rid of some of the excess energy, she took an early ride on her old bike. She rode several miles—for well over an hour—and she did a lot of thinking and praying as she did.

She returned to her mother's house tired, sweating, and a lot clearer in her mind than she'd been in a long time.

She was also a little sad. Sad but determined.

Her mother was awake, drinking tea and knitting in her favorite recliner by the window, when Betsy came back into the house.

"Do you want any breakfast?" her mother asked. "I can make you something."

"I'm fine. Don't get up."

"Well, get a banana. You need vitamins after all that exercise."

Betsy chuckled, but she grabbed a banana and a bottle of water before she sank into a chair next to her mother in the small living room.

She felt her mother studying her in a way that was very familiar.

"How are your knees?" Betsy asked.

"Not bad this morning. How are you feeling?"

"Good. I feel pretty good."

"What are your plans for the day?"

"They're pretty flexible. I can take you grocery shopping this morning if you want. And then I'll probably visit John this afternoon."

Her mother made a humming sound but didn't reply in words.

Betsy tightened her lips. "Don't start, Mom. Please."

"I'm not starting anything."

"I know what you're thinking."

"It wouldn't bother you the way it does if you didn't know I'm right."

Of course her mother was right. She almost always was. That was one of the conclusions Betsy had come to this morning. She sighed deeply and leaned back in her chair, closing her eyes as she admitted, "I know. I *know*. But John isn't just my boss. He's my friend, and he was pushed into this thing against his will. I can't just abandon him."

"No one is expecting you to abandon him. But you also need to do what's best for you."

"I'm going to. I mean, I need to think more about what that will look like, but I'm going to try to think of the future as well as what's working for me right now. And you're right. At the moment, I really am happy. I love my work, and I feel like I'm really contributing something important. I don't feel alone because I have so much community with my team. With John. But if—when—John gets married, things are going to feel a lot different for me. I didn't think I was... I was holding out any hope or daydreams or... I mean, I've never let myself think like that about him. But John said something to me yesterday that really drove things home to me."

She hadn't intended to spill so much of her personal feelings, and now she felt a little embarrassed about it—even with her mother.

"What did he say?"

Betsy shook her head, still feeling a pang of pain at the memory of John's curt words the day before. "It was nothing really. He was annoyed and said something thoughtless. That I wasn't his boss or his girlfriend and so I had no say on his life. He didn't mean it to… hurt the way it did. It shouldn't have hurt my feelings so much."

Her mother frowned. "He shouldn't speak to you that way."

"I know. He felt bad right away about it. But it shouldn't have hurt me so much. It just drove home the fact that, in some way, we're kind of acting like a couple—just like you said the other day. Without any romance or… or anything between us, but still… I don't think there's anything wrong with it necessarily, but it's not good for me emotionally."

"I think that's right, honey. I'm sure it's a hard thing to deal with, but I think you'll be better off if you try to… shake things up."

"That's what I'm going to do. I don't know about my job. I really don't want to give it up. But maybe I will. Or maybe I'll find other ways to… to find the distance I need."

"So maybe you don't go see John every day?"

"I promised him I would. No matter what, he's important to me."

"I know, honey. But you're just as important as he is. And you can't keep visiting him if it hurts you."

"Yesterday was just a fluke. He's really a great guy. He would never hurt me on purpose."

"Of course not. I know he wouldn't. But he doesn't have to intend it for it to happen. Men…" She trailed off as if she second-guessed speaking her mind.

"Men what?" Betsy prompted, genuinely curious, despite her lingering angst about the decisions she needed to make.

"Men don't always know what they do to us. And so they'll keep taking what's offered because we keep giving without getting what we need in return."

For some reason the quiet words caused a lump of emotion to tighten in Betsy's throat.

She was thirty now. She was smart and organized and good at her job. She was practical and reasonable and generally made good decisions. She was content. She was happy. She felt like in most ways she had her life together.

And yet she still found herself in the same kind of emotional situations she'd been in all through high school and college. Accepting less than what she really wanted from a man even if it hurt her.

Finally her throat relaxed enough for her to say quietly, "I didn't realize… I haven't been yearning for him all this time. I haven't been that silly."

"I know, honey."

"But I guess maybe it was always there at the back of my mind."

"That's perfectly natural and normal. Any other woman in your situation would probably have felt the same way. John is a good, decent man, and he's quite a looker too."

Betsy couldn't help but giggle at her mother's choice of words. "A looker?"

Her mother's eyes widened. "Isn't he?"

"Yes, he is." Despite herself, Betsy was starting to feel better. She always felt better when decisions were made, when she could see some sort of plan for her future—no matter what it was. "I can't just stop seeing him altogether for the next two weeks though."

"Of course not. But maybe you can start filling your mind with something else as well. Eileen told me yesterday that her nephew just moved to Nag's Head. He took over a dental practice there. He's around forty and was divorced a few years ago. She says he's a good Christian man."

"Mom—"

"Don't Mom me. He doesn't know anyone in the area. I'm sure he'd like a nice girl to show him around."

Betsy groaned.

"It will give you something else to think about," her mother added.

That was true. She had no desire to go out with some strange guy, but maybe it was a good idea to do it, just to show herself new possibilities in her world.

"Okay," she said at last. "If you and Eileen want to fix us up and the guy is willing, then I'd be okay with that."

Her mother smiled. "Excellent. You always were a very smart girl."

A smart girl.

That was Betsy.

Smart. Practical. Organized. Reliable.

Basic.

Boring.

Not the kind of girl who guys daydreamed about.

~

She had a surprisingly good morning—shopping with her mother and then going to a cute sandwich shop on the beach for lunch.

She arrived at Balm in Gilead at about one forty-five, and when she asked the glowering Zeke where to find John, she was told curtly, "Studio." He pointed down a hall on the first floor, so she wandered in that direction.

She peeked into the rooms she passed until she saw John in a big room at the end of the hall.

It was indeed a studio, filled with several easels and a couple of big drafting tables. There were a few people working in the room, including John—who was standing in front of a canvas on an easel and scowling as he stroked a paintbrush across it.

She'd known that guests were required to participate in five creative activities each week, but she'd never expected to see John painting.

She walked over quietly, curious about what she would see on his canvas.

He turned his head and saw her, and then he moved forward to block her before she could see.

"Hey!" she objected. "I wanted to see."

"It's none of your business."

"That's not very nice." She was smiling now because, despite his scowl, she could tell he wasn't annoyed with her.

"Tough."

"Why won't you show me?"

"Because it sucks."

"I'm sure it doesn't suck."

"It sure as hell does."

"Why did you decide to paint?"

"What else am I supposed to do? I wasn't about to join a sing-along or ramble endlessly in a journal."

She chuckled. "Don't they have dance lessons?"

He scowled even more deeply at her, causing her to burst into laughter.

"Please let me see," she begged playfully.

"Maybe after it's done. I'm supposed to do this for ten more minutes, or I can't check it off for the week."

She nodded, pleased that he was taking the requirements seriously. "I'll go wander around and come back. But you have to let me see it when you're done."

She heard him muttering as she left the room, "I have to do no such thing."

She was smiling as she went back to the hall. She found a chair in the lobby and killed time by texting Nancy, her best friend on the team.

It was two o'clock before she realized it, and she slipped her phone in her small purse and went back to the studio.

John was still working. He seemed so focused that she was able to sneak in silently and was behind him before he realized it.

He jerked and tried to block her view when he became aware of her presence, but this time she was able to see the canvas.

"Oh, it's good!" she exclaimed.

"No, it's not." He curled up his lip as he gave up trying to block her view.

"It is good."

"You don't have to lie to me."

"I'm not lying. You're not some sort of secret genius painter, but it's way better than I could do."

She studied the painting seriously, her first impression confirmed the longer she looked at it.

He'd painted the beach—ocean waves, sand dunes, and lots of blue sky. There was someone in the distance, walking on the beach, although the figure was too vague to identify. If the painting was supposed to be purely representational, then it wouldn't have been great—because so many of the lines were blurred or fuzzy. But the overall effect was quite nice.

"I like it."

He was studying her face carefully, and he must have finally concluded she was speaking the truth. "Thanks," he mumbled. "I wouldn't have done it if I didn't have to."

"I know. But did you enjoy painting it at all?"

He gave a half shrug. "It wasn't terrible."

"I guess that's better than nothing."

She was smiling as she helped him clean his supplies and move the canvas to the other side of the studio to dry, freeing up the easel for someone else to use.

"Sorry I had to finish that up," he said as they left the room together. "I hope I didn't waste most of the time you have to visit me today."

The words were bland, perfectly normal conversation, but she felt her cheeks warming slightly at the implication that he didn't want to miss out on his time with her.

Just another sign that she didn't have nearly enough emotional distance with him. It wasn't good for her heart.

She mentally squared her shoulders and gave him a casual smile. "I'm not really on a schedule today."

"Oh. Good."

"What did you want to do?"

"I don't know. What do you want to do?"

It wasn't like him to be indecisive. He nearly always had an opinion about things—often a very strong opinion. She wasn't sure if she liked the change or was worried by it.

"What have you done so far today?"

"I ran this morning. And then I read, had lunch, and painted."

She didn't ask him what he read since that had led to the argument yesterday. "Have you walked on the beach at all?"

His brows drew together. "I ran on the beach."

"I know that. I meant walking—just for fun. To feel the sand between your toes. You painted a picture of someone doing that, but you haven't done it yourself?"

"Why is that such a big deal? I like to run."

It seemed so characteristic of him to choose to run—working himself hard, doing something that felt productive—rather than just relax and enjoy himself. It bothered her a lot. "Of course you do. But let's go walk."

He still seemed confused at her reaction, but he didn't object. They walked out the back doors, by the pool, and then down the walkway to the beach.

The breeze was a little cooler than yesterday, but the sun was bright and it was quite comfortable. When they got to the wet sand, she leaned over and took off her sandals.

John just stood and watched her until she gave him a significant look.

With a sigh, he toed his shoes off and then bent over to pick them up. "What's the big deal?"

"The big deal is that it's nice and there's no reason for you not to enjoy it."

"Fine. I'll enjoy it." He sounded rather crabby.

She was torn between giggling and scowling, but the giggling won out.

They walked through the rise and fall of the tide in silence for several minutes, and Betsy enjoyed the feel of the breeze, the warmth of the sun, the tickling of the moving sand, the sounds of birds and waves. The beach wasn't very crowded—dotted with the occasional walker, runner, or fisher.

It was a good thing she'd come to a few hard decisions this morning because otherwise she might get lost in the fact that walking on the beach with John like this felt private, intimate, special.

She wasn't going to fall into traps like that though.

"Is something different about you?" he asked after several minutes of silence.

She blinked. Could he possibly have read her mind and realized all the conclusions she'd come to that morning? "What do you mean?" It was mostly a stall question, but she had no idea what else to say.

"I don't know. Something looks different about you. Did you do something different with your hair... or something?" He was staring at her, more questioning than admiring.

She'd tried out a little makeup this morning. Not for John. But because she'd wanted to see if she could pull it off, see if she could feel a little different about herself. She was startled that John had even noticed it.

Of course, he had assumed it was her hair. "I always wear my hair this way," she said, patting her ponytail.

"Yeah. I guess so. Just something seemed different." His brow was wrinkled, and she knew he was still trying to figure it out—but evidently the makeup was so subtle he couldn't pinpoint what was making the difference. "You always wear your hair like that?"

She couldn't hold back a laugh. "Yes, Sherlock. I always wear the same ponytail."

"Why?"

He seemed genuinely interested and not like he wanted her to fix her hair in a different style, so she wasn't self-conscious or defensive about the question. "I don't know. It's just easy and keeps my hair off my face so it doesn't bother me."

"Why would it bother you?"

"If I'm working or focusing or something, it falls down over my shoulders."

"You're not working now."

"Yeah. I suppose."

"What does it look like when it's down? I can't believe I don't even know this." He was still gazing at her face, but his expression had changed.

She couldn't specify the difference, but her cheeks began to flush. "It looks like... hair."

"Show me."

"What?"

"You heard me. Show me."

She reached up slowly to the elastic band and, feeling like an idiot, slid it out of her hair. Her hair was plain old light brown, but it was thick and smooth. It fell down around her neck and shoulders in a heavy cascade.

John's face changed again, and she could have sworn she saw admiration. She'd never seen that in his eyes when he looked at her before. "There's a lot of it," he said rather gruffly.

She smothered an ironic laugh. No way to hold on to silly daydreams when John was around. He always brought her back to reality very quickly. "What did you expect?"

"I don't know. It doesn't look like that much when it's up."

She sighed and smoothed her hair down. She was tempted to pull it back in its normal ponytail, but she didn't.

"Did you always wear the ponytail?" he asked after a minute.

"Why are you all of a sudden obsessed with my hair?"

"What else do I have to think about?"

She thought about this and then nodded. "I've worn it since... high school?"

"Even back then?"

"Yes."

"Why?"

It was the same question he'd asked before, but she knew he wanted the deeper answer. She hesitated briefly before she admitted, "I guess I never thought I was very pretty, so I didn't want to look like I was trying."

His eyes widened. "Why did you think that?"

"Because I wasn't. I mean, I wasn't ugly or anything. I was just... plain. Kids would sometimes call me 'Basic Betsy.'"

"What? Why?" He looked almost outraged at the old nickname.

"It wasn't an insult. Not really. I was just always... basic. Nothing special. So I didn't want to embarrass myself by trying to look in a way I couldn't really be. I don't know if that makes any sense."

"It makes sense. It's just not rational."

She slanted him an annoyed look. "I know it's not rational. Insecurities never are. That's how I felt. I never tried to work very hard on my appearance because I didn't want to be disappointed when I wasn't pretty at the end of it."

"But you *are* pretty," he said. The words were blunt, obviously not spoken to make her feel better.

"I think I probably improved with age."

"Or you were pretty all along and just didn't know it."

"Maybe." She was blushing again, but there was no way she could stop herself. She always did when she was self-conscious or embarrassed, and now she was both.

"I didn't realize you were insecure," he said after a few moments, softly, like he was speaking to himself.

"Everyone is about something. I've gotten better about it. It's just that I've never thought I was... one of those women."

"Which women?"

The ones men were attracted to, the ones men fell in love with.

She wasn't prepared to give that answer to John though, so she said, "The pretty ones."

"That's stupid."

She rolled her eyes. "I can always count on you for kind words."

He obviously knew she was being sarcastic, but he answered her seriously, "You can always count on me for *true* words."

"Yeah. I know."

They walked in silence for several minutes after that, each of them lost in their own thoughts.

After a long time, John murmured, "This hardly feels like the real world. Don't you think?"

She turned to look at him and was hit with a wave of attraction at the sight of his brown hair and tanned skin in the golden sunlight, his blue eyes deep with the reflection of the ocean, his lean body warm and strong and *right there*.

She swallowed over the feeling and pushed it down. "What do you mean?"

"This feels so far away from the real world, all the things we normally deal with, all the... all the hard things. It doesn't feel real."

The words hurt her strangely. She raised a hand to her chest unconsciously. "It does feel far away from all that. But this is the real world too."

He gazed down at her, and she had no idea what he was thinking.

She continued, focusing on the ideas rather than the sight of John so close to her. "The real world isn't just the hard things. It's the good things too."

"Yeah." His reply felt automatic rather than genuine.

"It is."

"I know. Of course."

She wondered if he really did know. He certainly didn't act like it. In a way, she could understand since he'd committed his life to doing anything he could to make the hard things better. Those were the things that would feel the realest to him.

But the result was he'd seemed to cut himself off from the rest, the enjoyment, the pleasures of life. She'd never realized it before—not the way she could see it now.

He smiled a lot and laughed a lot and seemed content as he did his job. It wasn't like he lived his life constantly unhappy. But he couldn't seem to let go, surrender, give in to simple enjoyments if they didn't have constructive purpose.

She wondered why she hadn't seen it before.

It worried her.

"What's the matter?" he demanded after they'd walked in silence for a few more minutes.

"It's nothing." The denial was automatic since obviously she couldn't tell him what she'd been thinking. He would hate that she'd had such thoughts about him.

"I'm trying to do better," he said, stopping again and looking down at her.

For no good reason her breath caught in her throat. "What do you mean?"

"I'm trying to do better—in staying here, in… in downtime. I'm trying to do better. I'm working on it."

Of course he was. He was *trying*. He was *working*.

She wanted to do something, to say something, to address what she'd sensed in him. But there was nothing really she could say.

And it wasn't her place.

He wasn't her boyfriend. They weren't in an intimate relationship.

He was her boss and maybe—sometimes—her friend. She needed to do better at keeping her heart in the right place.

"I know," she said at last with another casual smile. "I'm glad."

His brows had lowered, wrinkling his forehead, and he was peering at her face.

She turned away and started walking again.

He fell into step with her, and they talked about conversational things—her mother, their coworkers, the people he'd seen and met at the center.

She didn't have any more of those deep feelings of intimacy or waves of attraction for him, so she considered the visit a success.

FOUR

The following morning, John found himself looking forward to Betsy's visit.

A lot.

So much that he started to wonder about himself.

He wasn't the kind of guy who was used to taking it easy, so he found the forced relaxation rather frustrating and boring, and maybe he'd be happy to see anyone known and familiar. But still...

He couldn't remember ever being so excited to see someone else before. He kept thinking about her all morning, imagining what she would look like, what she would say, whether she would feel as strangely distant as she did yesterday, whether she would wear her hair in a ponytail.

It was honestly a little unsettling.

He ate breakfast alone and ran on the beach the way he'd done the day before. Then he showered and read on the patio. He still hadn't finished his theology book, but instead, he read one of the paperback novels Betsy had brought him.

It was a spy novel. Predictable but entertaining. Not bad at all.

He still found himself glancing at his watch every few minutes to check the time and wonder when Betsy would arrive.

She better come. He wouldn't vouch for the state of his mood if she didn't.

He'd made himself focus on his book and was getting into it again when he became aware of a presence beside him.

He looked up and saw Betsy.

She was smiling and shockingly pretty in a pale blue sundress. Her hair was loose today but brushed out so it was soft, and the sun burnished the light brown to gold.

He stared up at her speechlessly, both his heart and his body tightening at the unexpected sight of her standing next to him.

She lowered herself to sit sideways on the chaise next to his. "You're reading a novel!"

He blinked a few times and tried to make his mind work. What the hell had gotten into him that he was reacting to her this way? "You're early."

That wasn't at all what he'd intended to say. In fact, it had come out rather gruff, like he wasn't happy to see her.

Her smile faltered slightly. "Is it not a good time?"

He shook himself off and closed his book. "Sure. It's fine. I'm just reading."

Her eyes scanned his face closely. "I've got something else planned for this afternoon, so I thought I'd come see you earlier than normal if that's all right."

His immediate thought was that she better not have plans with some other guy—not looking as pretty as she was. What he said was, "You're all dressed up. Did you decide to try something new at last?"

"Kind of. I mean, obviously, I'm wearing a dress and my hair is down. But it's not just to try it out. My mom wants me to go to this garden party this afternoon, so I thought I'd drive straight there after visiting you."

John relaxed at hearing this. A garden party with a bunch of old people shouldn't be any problem. "Sounds exciting."

Betsy laughed softly. "Oh, it should be. She's trying to fix me up with the son of one of her friends."

John stiffened in indignation again. "What?"

"She's trying to fix me up." Betsy looked a little surprised by his tone. "The nephew of her friend is going to be at this party, so I'm required to meet him."

"Just tell her you're not interested."

"I haven't even met the guy yet. I don't know if I'm interested or not."

John glowered, liking the sound of this less and less. "Who is this loser?"

Now Betsy was frowning at him. "Why do you assume he'd be a loser?"

"His aunt is trying to set him up, isn't she?"

"That doesn't mean anything. My mom is trying to set me up. Am I a loser too?"

John realized he'd made a mistake. A number of them. Betsy was upset and offended. "That's different," he muttered.

"How exactly is it different?"

The only answer he had was that she was Betsy, and she was obviously not a loser, but that didn't feel like something that could be said. He just sat and scowled at the thought of her meeting some guy, looking like that.

The man would fall in love with her in an instant.

Maybe she'd fall in love with him too.

Then she'd quit her job, and John would never see her again.

He couldn't stand the thought of it.

"Why are you in such a bad mood today?" she asked after a minute.

"I'm not in a bad mood."

"Could have fooled me."

"Sorry."

"Are you?" She was peering at him again, and it made him uncomfortable. She definitely couldn't be reading his mind at the moment. He was thinking a number of inappropriate thoughts.

"Yes. I am."

They frowned at each other for a few moments, and then she relaxed with a little smile. "No wonder you never relax if it makes you this grumpy. No one could stand to be around you."

"I'm not grumpy."

She laughed again, looking so bright and amused that he couldn't help but smile back.

"It's almost time for lunch," he said, telling himself to get a grip on himself and not act like a complete fool. "You want to eat with me?"

"Sure. I haven't had anything."

They walked to the dining room, and he was hit with a very unusual feeling of self-consciousness as they entered. It felt like everyone was staring at him, speculating about his relationship with Betsy.

It was no one's business what his relationship with Betsy was.

He wasn't even sure what it was himself.

He'd always considered them coworkers, but he was obviously feeling more than that.

He wasn't even sure where the feelings had come from.

This was the problem with taking a vacation. Without work to occupy his thoughts, they drifted off in unexpected and inappropriate directions.

After they got their food from the buffet, he headed directly to his normal table for two next to the window. Betsy was looking around as she sat across from him.

"You don't want to join the big group?" she asked.

"I haven't really been in the mood to socialize." When he realized he sounded grumpy and Betsy's brows were pulling together, he added quickly, "With anyone except you."

She gave him a little smile. "That sounds reasonable to me. You're supposed to be resting, after all."

He wished he weren't in the position of being so needy and pathetic. He much preferred Betsy to think he was strong, in control.

He wasn't sure what he could do about it though, so he let the comment go without a response.

Betsy must have read something into his silence. "Are you still mad about it?"

"Mad about what?"

"About us kind of tricking you into coming here."

"There was no *kind of* about it."

Damn it. That was the wrong thing to say too. What was wrong with him lately? He was usually good with people. Opinionated, sure. But they usually liked him.

"I'm not mad," he added quickly.

"You sound like you are."

"Well, I'm not. It's okay. I understand."

She was eyeing him closely. "We were worried about you."

"I know."

"It's not an indictment, you know. It doesn't mean you're somehow not up to the job. It just means... we were worried."

He sighed and rubbed his face with his hands. "I know."

"It just means we care about you."

He liked the sound of her saying those words. He almost wished she'd said *I* instead of *we*. "I know," he said again, rather gruffly this time.

"And we were also worried the whole team would quit and we couldn't find anyone else willing to work with you," Betsy added in a different, teasing tone.

Despite himself, John chuckled at the quick change in mood. "I wasn't that bad."

Betsy just arched her eyebrows in an adorably wry expression.

"Okay. Maybe I was."

"You do seem better," she said. "It's been a long time since I've really heard you laugh."

He was sure that wasn't true. He must have laughed recently. But, searching his memory, he couldn't really remember.

Because he didn't really know what to say, he asked, "You want me to say grace?"

Betsy nodded, and he gave quick thanks for the food before they started eating.

They'd only taken a few bites when John was distracted by a raised voice on the other side of the room.

At the table was a woman he'd met briefly as they'd been painting this morning. Marie. A middle-aged woman who was going through a divorce.

The man at the table with her must be her ex-husband. The look on their faces and the tension evident between them testified to this fact.

As he watched, the man shouted at Marie something about how he was going to make sure she came back to him. John only vaguely registered the words. What he noticed was the loud, harsh sound and the way Marie shrank into her seat, looking frightened, almost paralyzed. She had become the center of attention in the room, and that seemed to bother her as much as her ex-husband's shouting.

John immediately rose to his feet. He wasn't thinking—just reacting. A man didn't get to speak to a woman that way. Not in his presence. He simply wouldn't allow it.

He'd only taken two steps toward them, however, when another man intervened.

Zeke had appeared out of nowhere, wearing bright orange shorts and a faded brown T-shirt, and had grabbed the man by the back of his shirt and hauled him to his feet.

Marie's ex-husband wasn't a small man, so it was a notable feat of strength.

"Let go of me!" he demanded, struggling in Zeke's grip.

Zeke didn't reply in any way. He just pushed the other man toward the door.

"Zeke." An authoritative female voice broke into the shocked silence of the dining room.

Cecily was standing near the doorway, looking just as polished and feminine as ever.

Zeke glanced back at his boss.

John noticed she didn't look worried or upset about the outburst. Mostly she looked just slightly impatient.

"Use your words, please," she added, clearly still speaking to Zeke.

Zeke scowled at the man who was struggling in his grip. "Get the fuck out of here," he growled.

John had to smother an instinctive laugh at the way Zeke chose to "use his words." He glanced over to Betsy, who had moved to stand beside him, and they shared a smile that was strangely warm, strangely intimate.

When he looked back over at Cecily, he could see quickly suppressed amusement on her face too, but her voice was cool as she arched her eyebrows at Zeke. "Use better words, please."

Zeke was walking Marie's ex-husband to the door, so his words were rather redundant as he said roughly, "Get out of here, and don't come back."

Marie herself was red with what looked like mortification, but she thanked Zeke and apologized to Cecily, both of whom just brushed off her taking responsibility for her ass of an ex-husband.

Gradually the feeling in the room returned to normal, and John and Betsy went back to their table.

John was eating his sandwich and salad—enjoying the sandwich a lot more than the salad—when Betsy asked, "Have you learned anything more about Zeke?"

John paused, his fork in the air. "What do you mean?"

"I mean exactly what I asked. Have you talked to Zeke in the past couple of days? Have you learned anything more about him?"

"Why do you want to know?"

She was obviously surprised by his question. "I was just wondering. He's an interesting man."

"He's not that interesting." He wasn't sure why he was feeling so defensive, but he didn't like Betsy's obvious interest in someone as rude and antisocial as Zeke.

"Yes, he is. Why doesn't he like to talk? And why does he dress so strange. Did you see those shorts?"

"Some people just have bad taste."

"I guess, but still… There's a story there, and I'm interested in it."

"I don't think he's in the market for a wife," John muttered.

Betsy's eyes went very round. "I wasn't wanting to date him! I was just curious."

The tension in his chest relaxed at her obvious surprise. "I haven't talked to him," he replied in a more natural tone. "What we heard from him just now seems to be the extent of his ability to converse."

"Do you not like him for some reason?"

Honestly, the only reason John felt negative vibes toward the other man was because Betsy had wanted to know more about him. Since this was obviously irrational and inappropriate, he wasn't going to admit to it. "I don't know anything about him."

She still looked confused, vaguely questioning, but fortunately she didn't pursue the topic. "Okay."

They ate in silence for a few minutes, and John's mind returned quite frustratingly to how pretty Betsy looked across from him. Her hair kept falling in front of her shoulders, and she would push it back impatiently.

He found himself wanting to touch it, to see if it was as soft as it looked.

"So why isn't this guy at work in the afternoon?" he demanded out of the blue.

She blinked. "What? Zeke is at work. He works here."

John cleared his throat, realizing he'd very stupidly spoken his thoughts out loud. "Not him. This guy they're trying to fix you up with. Why is he at a garden party on a weekday afternoon and not at work? He does have a job, doesn't he?"

"Yes, he has a job. He's a dentist. He doesn't have office hours on Wednesday afternoons."

Naturally, he would be a dentist. He probably had a very successful practice. Why else would her mother be trying to fix Betsy up with him? "Of course he doesn't."

"What does that mean?"

"Nothing."

"You don't need to be snide about it. I haven't met him yet, but evidently, he's really nice and smart. He's a good Christian, and everyone likes him a lot."

John already resented this nice, smart, good Christian dentist whom everyone liked a lot.

"Why didn't you tell your mother you're not interested in meeting him?" he asked.

Betsy's forehead was wrinkled with a baffled frown. "Why do you assume I'm not interested in meeting him?"

Damn it. He was making a mess of this conversation too. Maybe he did need a rest. He just couldn't pull it together. "I just mean it's kind of awkward to be fixed up that way. You could have just told her you weren't interested. We'll be going back in the field next month anyway, so it's not like there's much future for a relationship."

Betsy seemed to grow very still, and she didn't answer his question.

Her silence, her stillness, frightened him more than anything else would have.

He suddenly knew she was rethinking her job.

Maybe she didn't want to stay on the team with him.

Maybe she wanted to get married to some nice, smart dentist and have a passel of kids.

Maybe she didn't want to work with him—to be with him—anymore.

He couldn't stand the thought of it. It prompted a flare of panic in his mind that he couldn't quite control.

Both of them were silent for a long time. He had no idea what Betsy was thinking, but he was struggling to gain control of the twisting in his heart, in his gut, at the thought of Betsy leaving him for a very different life.

Nothing would be the same again.

Finally he couldn't stand the silence any longer, so he tried to speak in a natural, casual tone. He wasn't successful. "I thought you were happy in the job."

"I am," she said, her own voice breaking slightly as if her reflections had made her emotional too. "I am happy. But I have to think in… in the long-term."

Of course she did. Anyone in her position would. Their jobs were hard and exhausting and draining and sometimes dangerous. Most people didn't do this work forever.

"I didn't know you wanted to get married," he said, hoping he didn't sound as upset by this idea as he felt.

She gave a little shrug and stared at her plate. "I… I'm happy the way I am, but I don't want to completely close down the possibility. I mean, I'd be content if it never happens, but if…" She cleared her throat. "I just want to be open to possibilities."

"Of course."

"I'm not husband hunting or anything," she added.

He'd been staring out the window, but at this his eyes shot back over to her face. "I never thought you were."

"I just…"

"You don't have to explain yourself, Betsy. I'm sorry I sounded so... so discouraging. If you want to meet this guy, then you should."

He didn't mean the words, but they were the ones he needed to say. They were the right ones.

"I'm not expecting a gallant knight on a white horse," Betsy said with something closer to her normal smile.

"I never thought you were. That doesn't really seem to be your thing."

He'd just been feeling better, more himself, ready to move on to their usual comfortable interaction. But evidently, he'd said the wrong thing again.

Her shoulders stiffened slightly. "Why wouldn't it be my thing? I can be romantic."

"I didn't mean you couldn't. I'm sorry. It was supposed to be a compliment. I just meant you don't seem prone to silly daydreams."

She was smiling again, but it didn't reach her eyes— like something was still bothering her. "I guess I'm not anymore."

"Did you used to be?" This was something he'd never known about her, and he wanted to know more.

"Yes. I suppose. I mean, when I was a girl, I had all the normal romantic daydreams."

"A knight on a white horse?"

"Don't laugh. He wasn't really a knight in my daydreams, and the horse wasn't white. It was a gray horse. But he did ride up on the horse and give me a big bunch of flowers."

"Seriously?"

"Don't laugh." She was relaxing now, and her eyes were fond and amused. "I was a little girl. It seemed the most romantic thing in the world to me back then." She sighed deeply. "I guess we all grow up."

John was suddenly hit with a feeling of intense injustice—on her behalf. It wasn't right—it was simply wrong—that Betsy hadn't had that kind of daydream romance.

He hadn't realized she'd wanted it.

It had never even crossed his mind.

Betsy's cheeks were delicately flushed and her eyelids lowered, and John was momentarily mesmerized by how lovely she looked.

He sure hoped the good, smart dentist didn't get to see her looking like this.

"Anyway," she said in more of her normal tone. "I don't daydream much anymore. I'm a pretty practical person, you know."

"I know. I like that about you."

She seemed pleased by the compliment, but the softness was gone from her eyes.

He wanted it back.

"What did you do this morning?" she asked, clearly wanting to get back to normal conversation.

"Ran. Painted. Read."

"What did you paint today?"

He gave a little shrug. He was actually enjoying painting more than he would have expected, but it seemed like a silly thing to enjoy. Not really like him.

"Let me see it," she demanded.

They'd both finished their lunches by now, and Betsy was standing up, clearly intent on seeing the product of his creativity this morning.

There wasn't really any sense in arguing. With a sigh, he got up too. They picked up their dishes, dropped them off at the window to the kitchen, and then walked down the hall to the studio.

She glanced around and evidently picked out his painting immediately. She walked over to it unerringly.

"How did you know this one was mine?" he asked, feeling a little self-conscious as if she knew his heart better than he'd realized.

"It just looks like you. I like it." She was smiling as she stared at the painting, which was of two sets of legs hanging down from a fishing pier and two rods cast into the water.

"Thanks. It's not that great."

"It's good. I like it."

"Thanks," he mumbled, pleased and embarrassed both.

"You should go fishing this afternoon," she said. "It's obviously on your mind, so you should do it."

"I'll do it if you come with me." He spoke the words spontaneously, just liking the idea of fishing with her.

"I can't. I have that garden party."

Shit. The good, smart dentist. "Right. Oh well."

She gave him a little smile.

"You could always skip it," he said, responding to the surprisingly strong urge to spend the whole afternoon with her. "The dentist can wait."

For a moment she looked tempted. He really thought she might agree.

But then her features twisted, like she'd come to some sort of internal conclusion, and she shook her head. "I better not. I promised my mom I'd be there."

"Okay." He wasn't going to keep arguing. That would reveal far too much about the ways in which he was thinking about her. "Just an idea."

"You should still fish though. Do it for me."

"Okay. Sure."

He said the words mostly so she wouldn't keep pushing for it, but because he'd said he would do it, he felt obliged to do so.

After he walked Betsy out to her car and watched her drive away, he went to find Zeke and ask about fishing rods.

Then he walked out on the pier, sat down, and threw out his line.

He didn't catch anything, but it wasn't a bad afternoon.

It would have been a lot better, however, if he hadn't kept thinking about Betsy meeting that dentist.

What if she came to visit him tomorrow with her eyes full of stars and hearts for the loser? What if she'd decided this dentist was her silly knight on the gray horse?

John wouldn't like that at all.

FIVE

Betsy didn't sleep well that night, and she woke up early again, so she took another long bike ride before breakfast.

She tried to focus her mind as she rode—thinking through possibilities for the future and how nice Dennis, the man she'd met the day before, had been.

Instead, she'd spent the hour trying not to think about John. How he'd acted the day before. How he'd almost sounded jealous. How he'd been looking at her differently.

She wasn't prone to flights of fancy or wishful thinking, and she kept telling herself she was imagining things. John wouldn't all of a sudden start thinking about her differently—not after so long of seeing her as only a coworker. A dress and loose hair couldn't possibly make that much difference.

He was at loose ends. So was she. That was all it was.

She'd come to her own conclusions this week about her life and her future. She wasn't going to go back just because he'd given her a few wistful looks yesterday.

When she returned to the house, her mother was up and making a pot of oatmeal.

"It's humid out there this morning," Betsy said, grabbing a couple of paper towels to wipe her face with.

"You were up early. Couldn't sleep?"

Betsy gave a little shrug. "Just woke up early."

Her mother gave her a sharp look that didn't miss anything. "I guess it's too much to hope you were up all night gushing over Dennis."

Betsy chuckled. "Not really. He was very nice though. I wouldn't mind seeing him again if he's interested."

"Eileen said he was. I think he'll be calling you."

"Good. That's good then."

She meant the words. And she tried to be excited about them.

She tried once again not to picture John's face as they'd shared that intimate smile of amusement at Zeke tossing that jerk out of the dining room yesterday.

"You don't have to go out with him if you don't want to, Betsy. I didn't mean to pressure you."

Betsy straightened up in surprise. "I'm not feeling pressured. Really. And I think it's a good idea that I do."

"But you'd rather go out with someone else."

She gave another little shrug, feeling young and rather foolish, which was unusual for her. "I don't know. I didn't think I had those feelings for John, but then they suddenly materialized out of nowhere. But you were totally right—right about everything. I'm not going to be silly about it. If he wanted something more with me, he would... he would do something about it."

Her mother nodded soberly. "He would."

"He's been... acting differently this week, which is getting my emotions going, I guess. But I'm sure it doesn't mean anything."

"He's used to having you around. He'll notice if you start to pull away."

That was true. Of course it was. And that likely explained everything Betsy had been noticing.

John would never consciously try to use her or take advantage of her, but she'd been his right hand for a long time. He would respond to a shift in their relationship.

It didn't mean he wanted something more with her.

She sighed deeply, trying to cool down and trying to dispel the ache of disappointment at this sensible realization. "If Dennis wants to go out, I'll definitely say yes. He was really nice—and not bad-looking."

Dennis had been kind of cute in a low-key, slightly balding way. He'd been earnest and intelligent and interested in everything she'd said. There was absolutely nothing wrong with him.

It wasn't his fault he wasn't John.

"It's worth a try. Maybe you'll find him more exciting once you get to know him better." Her mother obviously knew she wasn't incredibly enthusiastic about him, and she was trying to be supportive—as she always was.

Her mother never failed to be supportive. She also never failed to be smart about human nature.

It was worth listening to her since Betsy wasn't always as smart as she wanted to be.

～

Betsy went out to Balm in Gilead at about one that afternoon.

She actually considered not going at all, thinking it might be better for her emotional well-being to stay away, but she'd promised John she would visit him. She wasn't going to break her word.

She could manage to see him for a couple of hours without falling into dangerous thinking.

On her drive down, she got a call from John's brother, Mark.

The call was to her phone and not to John's, but she recognized the area code and knew it must be Mark.

"Betsy," Mark said when she answered. "It's Mark. John's brother."

She almost giggled at the idea that he'd need to explain himself. Of course she knew who Mark was. John talked about him all the time. Plus they'd just spoken a couple of days ago when Mark had called John's phone.

"Yes, yes, of course. How are you?"

"Good," he said. "I'm doing well. A little worried about John. How's he doing?"

"Pretty well, I think. He's at least resigned himself to being here for two weeks. And he's been in a better mood."

"Good. Is he relaxing at all, do you think?"

Betsy hesitated because she really wasn't sure what the answer to that question was.

"Is it that bad?" Mark prompted after a moment.

"Not bad," she replied in a rush. "I mean, he really is doing better than he was before. He doesn't seem nearly as stressed or... or on edge. It's just that I don't really know if he's actually relaxing or if he's just..."

"Just behaving better because he knows that people are worried about him."

"Exactly," she said. She'd parked her car in the lot but stayed in her seat to finish the conversation. "He doesn't like to be worried about."

"That I know." Mark paused for a moment before he continued, "I know how he feels. When I came home, after... I couldn't stand the thought that anyone was worried about me or treating me like I needed help. And my attempt to not need that help just made everything worse. I almost lost Sophie. I know I did."

Betsy's throat hurt unexpectedly at this admission, at how raw and naked it felt. She couldn't imagine going through

72

what Mark had gone through. She could well believe the toll it had taken on his marriage. "John says you're doing a lot better now though," she said at last, wishing there was some better way to answer what he'd told her.

Mark cleared his throat. "I think I am. I just mention it because I can understand why John doesn't want our help. We need to give it to him anyway."

"Of course. Of course we do." She felt a little sliver of guilt that she'd considered staying away this afternoon.

Mark sighed, like he was thinking things through as he spoke. "I guess he's told you about our family situation growing up."

Betsy opened her mouth, but nothing came out. John never told her much about his childhood, although Mark obviously thought he would have. She finally managed to say, "He's told me you two were orphaned as teenagers."

"Yeah. He's always felt... responsible."

"Responsible?" Betsy's voice cracked slightly.

"I mean, it was hard for both of us, of course. When our parents died, our uncle and aunt took us in, but... John was the one who really took care of me, took care of us. He always felt responsible. He's always been like that. He still is. He was a rock when I was captured. He called Sophie every week to check in on her, no matter where you all were in the world. And he's been there for me anytime I need him ever since I've gotten back. He knows how to take care of people, but he doesn't know how to be taken care of."

The words rang true to Betsy. They were exactly right. She knew this about John herself. She'd seen it in so many ways.

"I'm glad he has you," Mark added in a slightly different tone.

Betsy's cheeks flushed hot, even alone in her car. It sounded like Mark believed she was more to John than she actually was, but she wasn't sure how to address it. "He's been a good friend to me," she said at last.

"He relies on you a lot. I'm not sure he even knows how much."

Betsy wondered if this was true.

"Is he... is he having any fun, do you think?" Mark asked, still clearly just following the shifting of his thoughts.

The question hit Betsy strangely. She started to answer instinctively, saying, "I'm sure he's..." But she trailed off, suddenly knowing her first answer wasn't true. "I guess I don't know," she said at last, feeling heavy, poignant.

"He's always trying to be strong, to be good, to be what he's supposed to be. And I guess I just want him to be able to let go, have fun, just... just..."

"Enjoy life," she finished for him.

"Yes. Can you help him?"

Betsy had absolutely no idea what to say to that.

She finally managed to stammer, "I'll... I'm not sure what I can do, but... but I can try."

"Thanks." Mark sounded relieved, as if he'd needed to hear her say that. "That makes me feel better. I wanted to come visit John this weekend if you think it's a good idea."

"Of course it's a good idea! He'd love to see you."

"Oh good. I don't think Sophie can make it. Her grandfather's been sick, and she needs to the cover the bookstore on Saturday, but I might bring a friend with me."

"John will be thrilled. So you'll be here Saturday, you think?"

"That's what I'm thinking. I could spend the night out there and drive back on Sunday.

"That's great. Really great." Betsy was genuinely happy because she knew John would be happy to see his brother, but she was also a little relieved for herself—that she wasn't solely responsible for John's emotional well-being.

She felt pretty helpless in that regard and even more so after her conversation with Mark.

Mark had clearly said what he'd wanted to say, so they said goodbye and hung up. Betsy sat in her car and breathed deeply for a minute before she finally got out.

She'd walked in through the front door when Zeke suddenly materialized in front of her. She had no idea how he seemed to always show up out of nowhere.

Before she could even say hello, he nodded toward the side hallway. "In the studio," he muttered before walking away.

Betsy chuckled at this piece of loquacity and walked toward the studio to find John.

He was just leaving the room as she was halfway down the hallway, and he blinked in surprise at the sight of her. She saw his expression change, and it was impossible to misread it.

He was really happy to see her. Her heart fluttered at the knowledge.

"I thought you might be here earlier," he said, approaching her and looking casual and very attractive in a pair of jeans and a heather-gray T-shirt. For some reason his shoulders looked broader and his biceps looked stronger than normal. He just looked more *man* than usual.

"I—" She stopped herself when she realized she was about to apologize. "I'm here now."

"I'm glad." He gave her a slightly sheepish smile. "I didn't mean to sound ungrateful before. I'd just been waiting for you."

It shouldn't—it really, really shouldn't—make her feel so good to hear that, to know it was true. She's always just been someone John worked with. It was nice that he also wanted her company.

She wasn't going to read any more into it than that.

"What do you feel like doing?" he asked.

"I don't know. We could walk on the beach, I guess."

This was evidently agreeable because John led her outside by the back patio and down toward the beach. They were making their way across the soft, dry sand toward the damp sand that was firmer and easier to walk on when John suddenly reached out and caught something that was about to hit her in the face.

She'd been looking down at her feet as she walked, so she hadn't seen it approaching.

A Frisbee.

"Oh! I didn't even see that." She laughed breathlessly. "Thanks for catching it."

"No problem." John's eyes had searched her briefly, as if he was checking for damage, but now he was staring at the young men approaching them.

It must be one of those men who'd thrown the Frisbee.

"Sorry," one of them called out. "It got away from us."

"Be careful next time," John said, still bristling slightly at the near miss.

"It's fine," she told the young man who'd spoken. "No damage done. I haven't thrown a Frisbee in years."

The man was grinning as he reached them. He was obviously staying at Balm in Gilead too because he was heading toward the same walkway they'd just come down. "You can use it if you want. Zeke found it for me, so it's not even mine. Just bring it back. I don't want to get on Zeke's bad side."

Betsy laughed and promised they would. They waved as the men made their way back to the building.

"Stop frowning," Betsy told John, who was still holding on to the Frisbee.

"You could have been hurt."

"I wasn't hurt. It was an accident. It happens. You rescued me."

He was still frowning, although his expression relaxed slightly as he looked at her.

"Did you want to throw it?" Betsy asked, nodding down toward the Frisbee in his hand.

John shrugged. "I don't know."

Betsy remembered what Mark had asked about whether John had any fun.

It was a beautiful, sunny afternoon. Not even too hot, despite the humid morning.

She and John should do something simple, something fun. They could throw the Frisbee.

"I want to, so you have to do it with me."

"Okay. Fine with me."

Pleased with his easy acceptance, Betsy headed farther down the beach until they were in a good position. There were a few other people in sight—a couple walking in the distance, two women lying out on chaises—but for the most part they were alone.

Betsy had been serious about it being years since she'd played with a Frisbee. She missed John's first throw, and then when she lobbed it back, it ended up in the water and John had to fish it out.

Her next throws weren't much better.

She laughed at John's exaggerated complaints about her bad aim and at least improved her ability to catch it.

They threw it back and forth for about twenty minutes, and gradually Betsy's aim improved. She was enjoying herself, and she could tell John was too. She forgot all about her need to distance herself from him. She forgot all about Mark's dependence on her to make John feel better.

She just liked the feel of the sun and the breeze and the sound of John's laughter.

She'd been doing well for several throws in a row when she backslid and threw the Frisbee in entirely the wrong direction—and quite far away.

John groaned loudly. "You should have to go get that one," he said, obviously teasing.

It had been a very bad throw. "I will," she said and started for it.

"Hey," John objected, heading toward the Frisbee himself. "I was joking. I'll get it."

"I can get it." She picked up her speed.

"I said I'd get it." He started to jog.

So Betsy started to run.

They were coming from different directions for the Frisbee, but Betsy was slightly closer. She was practically sprinting over the sand to get there before he did—since it was the principle of the thing that she beat him, after all.

He gave an aggrieved roar when she grabbed the Frisbee just before he got there, and then he reached out to take it from her.

She managed to back away from his reach. When he started after her, she did the only sensible thing a person could do in that situation. She ran away from him.

He chased her.

She was in a good shape, but she'd never been a runner, and the sand just made it worse. She did the best she could to dart away from him, but she didn't have much chance of eluding him.

She was breathless and flushed and laughing helplessly when he managed to grab her around the waist.

They'd been running too quickly, and she lost her footing, so they both ended up tumbling to the sand.

She at least had her wits about her enough to tuck the Frisbee beneath her so he couldn't get it.

"Why are you so stubborn?" John demanded. He'd been laughing too, and his face was warm and damp with perspiration and soft in a way she almost never saw it.

"Why am *I* stubborn? You're the one who won't let me get the Frisbee!"

"I told you I could get it." He was still on the ground, halfway beside her and halfway on top of her. He was holding himself above her on straightened arms.

"I was the one who threw it."

"And I was the one who was supposed to catch it."

"There was no way you could catch that throw."

"I could have tried." He was gazing down on her, and she saw the exact moment when his expression changed from laughter to something else.

The something else was just as warm, just as alive but softer, more intense, breathtaking.

It was admiration and surprise and something like yearning. His eyes seemed to caress her face as his head started to lower toward hers.

Her breath caught in her throat as she stared up at him. Her heart hammered so powerfully it seemed to shake her whole body.

"Betsy," she heard him murmur.

She couldn't say anything at all. She could only gaze up at him as his face got nearer to hers.

Then he was kissing her. Their lips were pressing together. And it was so surprising and so exciting, and it felt so good that her mind pulsed in a heated blur.

He withdrew his lips slightly. Stared down at her. And then leaned into another kiss.

This time she couldn't stop herself from wrapping her arms around his neck, pulling him closer to her. He was hot and heavy and felt so strong, so firm. She loved the feel of his hardness beneath his shirt as one of her hands slid down his back.

She'd never expected to feel him this way.

He was totally into the kiss. His lips and tongue were eager and urgent, and one of his hands had tangled in her hair, which she'd left loose again today. Her body hummed in pleasure, in excitement, and it definitely wanted even more.

She gasped when their lips broke apart and tried to pull him back down on her.

But something had changed now. He was pulling away. Scrambling up to his knees, then to his feet.

And she was left in a confused, undignified sprawl on the sand, still throbbing from that kiss.

"Shit," he muttered, rubbing his face and turning away from her. "Shit, shit."

Well, that didn't sound very good.

She swallowed hard and tried to make her brain work again instead of roaring with the need to kiss him again, kiss him more.

"I'm…" John still had his back to her, but he'd lowered his hands now. She could see he was breathing deeply. His shoulders were rising and falling. "I didn't mean to do that."

"I… I know. It just happened." What else could she say? He'd obviously not set out to kiss her, and he was clearly upset that it had happened. She wasn't going to embarrass herself by admitting that she was glad it had. "These things happen."

What an absolutely ridiculous thing to say.

"It won't happen again."

Just perfect. Exactly what any girl would want to hear after a kiss like that.

She managed to get up. "It's fine. Don't worry about it."

"I'm obviously… out of it. I shouldn't have let that happen. I'm…" He cleared his throat. "I'm your boss."

For some reason that felt like a slap to her face, although she knew he hadn't meant it that way.

He *was* her boss. And as such he absolutely shouldn't be kissing her.

It had always felt like there was more to their relationship than just that.

He'd said he wasn't himself.

She *was* herself, but that evidently didn't matter. "I was part of it too," she said. "It's not the end of the world. We'll just move on."

He turned around and, for a moment, searched her face with an urgency she hadn't expected and didn't understand. Then he nodded.

Wanting to break the tension so she wouldn't reveal to him what she was feeling, she said lightly, "So no more kissing. We're agreed?"

"Agreed."

They acted like everything was fine as they walked back up the walkway. Betsy was still carrying the Frisbee.

But everything wasn't fine.

She was an idiot. A silly fool.

Because no matter how much she told herself to be smart and mature and accept the fact that John was never going to fall in love with her, she still let herself hope for a few minutes as they kissed.

And so now she was crushed when her hopes came to nothing.

He was her boss. For now, at least.

And there was a strange, heartbreaking kind of comfort in the fact that he didn't have to be her boss for much longer.

~

Betsy was tempted not to visit John the following day. She was still upset about the kiss, and everything felt awkward now between them.

But they'd never be able to stay friends if they couldn't get past this, so she summoned her courage and went to see him.

She would only stay for a little while. She'd get it over with quickly. Then gradually things would go back to normal between them.

John was reading outside in the sun again when she arrived just after lunch, and she paused to look at him, hit with a wave of attraction she really wished she didn't feel. He was such a good-looking man. Not classically handsome but with strong features, gorgeous eyes, golden-tanned skin, and a great, fit body. When he smiled, any girl's heart would skip a beat.

She wasn't silly or stupid. It was normal and natural to be attracted to him. She just needed to control it so she didn't end up letting her emotions run out of control.

Any more out of control than they already were.

Her mother was right. She couldn't start to give her heart when John had made it clear he didn't want it.

He glanced up from his e-reader and saw her standing in the doorway. He smiled and waved at her, but his expression wasn't quite as genuine as normal.

He was probably feeling awkward too.

She took a deep breath and squared her shoulders.

Get this over with. Now.

Now.

She finally took a step, and John got up and walked over to meet her. "Hey. Thanks for coming over."

"Why wouldn't I?"

He raised his eyebrows. "After yesterday, I wasn't sure."

"I thought we were going to move on from that."

"Yes. We are."

"So then what's the worry?" She smiled at him blandly, praying she looked as casual as she was trying to sound.

Her act must have been convincing because his features relaxed slightly. "No worry at all."

"Good."

"I can't stay very long this afternoon. I've got to take my mom to do some errands."

"That's fine. You want to walk down to the beach?"

She glanced at the walkway and realized how long it would take to walk down to the beach and then across the sand and then stay long enough to make the trek worth it. And then walk back.

She wasn't sure her bland, casual act would hold out that long. "I better not get sandy. Let's just hang out on the patio if that's okay."

"Sure."

They sat down in two chairs with the best view, and they made empty conversation about Betsy's mother and Mark and the weather.

And it was terrible. Painful. It felt like they were strangers.

Just yesterday they'd been kissing passionately. The day before they'd been sharing their feelings—for real.

And today everything was all wrong.

It felt so stilted and meaningless that Betsy finally couldn't take any more. She glanced at her watch and said, "Oh, I better get going."

John stood up immediately. His face was perfectly composed, but his eyes were searching her face, as if he were looking for something in her expression that he couldn't find. "Okay. Sure."

"Sorry I can't stay very long."

"No need to be sorry. I'll walk you out."

Betsy felt kind of sick as they made their way through the lobby and then down the front walk to the parking lot. Surely things would be better tomorrow. Surely it wouldn't always feel so terrible between them. She couldn't stand it if it was.

She was so lost in her disturbing thoughts that she nearly tripped on a pile of something that was on the edge of the sidewalk. She blinked and looked down, realizing it was a pile of weeds.

"Are you okay?" John asked, reaching out to catch her at her near stumble.

His arm around her felt so good that she immediately jerked away. In doing so, she kicked the pile of weeds even more, and about half of them caught a breeze and drifted across the immaculate lawn.

"Oh no," she murmured. "Look at the mess I've made."

"Don't worry about it. Zeke can pick them up again. He shouldn't have left the pile where people would trip on them."

Betsy gasped as she stared down at the tumbled weeds. "Zeke was working on them?"

"Yeah. Most of the morning. He was pulling them. He's evidently obsessive about this lawn."

"He pulls them by hand? Why doesn't he use weed killer?" Betsy's voice was hushed and horrified.

"Maybe he wants to be environmentally friendly. Who cares? What does it matter anyway?"

"Zeke is going to be so mad when he sees I've messed up his lawn!" Betsy leaned over and started collecting the weeds she'd kicked out of the pile.

John chuckled softly. "So let him be mad."

"I don't want that man mad at me." She was scrambling around, picking up as many as she could find. "John, don't just stand there. Help me before he sees what I've done!"

John was still laughing, but he stepped over and started picking up the weeds. Together they found nearly all of them, and both of them were chuckling when they had their hands full.

And Betsy was feeling better again. More natural. This was the John she knew. This was the John she...

"What the hell?" a voice growled from behind them.

She squealed in surprise and dropped her pile of weeds.

She turned around to find Zeke glaring at her.

"Hey," John said with a frown, his tone firm and defensive. "Don't use that tone with her."

Betsy couldn't help but feel a little thrill of pleasure at his jumping to her defense like that, but she didn't want the men to actually get in a fight. "I just accidentally kicked the pile of weeds, so we were picking them up again."

Zeke didn't say anything else, but he watched suspiciously as John dumped the weeds in his hands into the original pile.

"Don't look at her like that," John said in a growl that was almost worthy of Zeke himself. "She hasn't done anything wrong. No one is going to mess with your precious weeds."

For just a moment Betsy thought she caught a glint of amusement in Zeke's eyes, but it was gone before she could verify.

She took John's arm and led him away before he got even more annoyed.

"That guy is an ass," he muttered as they walked toward her car.

"It's the way he is. Just ignore him."

"There was no reason for him to talk to you that way."

"He talks to everyone that way."

"He doesn't get to talk to you that way."

Betsy shivered with pleasure again. She was still holding on to his arm, and it felt like they belonged together.

Just as friends, she reminded herself.

Just as *friends*.

But at least that terrible stilted awkwardness from earlier was gone. She could thank Zeke for that.

SIX

Two days later, on Saturday morning, John woke up at dawn and ran for a few miles on the beach before breakfast.

He pushed himself hard and was drenched in sweat when he limped back up the walkway from the sand, so he collapsed into a chaise by the pool to dry out a little before he dripped perspiration all over the floor of the building.

Despite his gasping exhaustion, his mind just wouldn't let down.

It would help if he wouldn't keep replaying that kiss with Betsy in his mind—and imagining it going even further—but he clearly wasn't disciplined enough to keep himself from those tantalizing lines of thought.

He'd always been good at controlling himself before. Surely he could pull it together again soon.

He was praying silently, staring up at the sky, asking for help in what he obviously couldn't do himself, when a voice behind him made him jerk.

"This doesn't look like rest to me."

He turned around to see Cecily smiling down at him, looking just as prim and polished in a skirt and heels as she always did, despite the early hour.

"I like to run," he replied. He liked Cecily and didn't want to be rude to her, even though he'd rather be left to himself.

She neatly lowered herself to sit on the side of the chaise beside him, facing him and still smiling. "This looks more like fleeing from demons than running for fun." Her voice was light and casual, despite the words.

He wiped some more sweat from his face with the back of his hand. "I don't have demons."

"We all have demons."

"Yeah. I guess. But mine are pretty... mild. I'm just not used to sitting still for so long, and I feel restless."

"I can understand that."

He gave her a sidelong look. He could tell she was thinking things about him that she wasn't saying, and it bothered him irrationally. "I'm really fine. I don't need counseling or anything."

"I didn't say you did. But you're welcome to it if you like. Others here have found it helpful."

"I'm sure they do. But most of them have... been through things that call for it."

"And you haven't?"

He drew his eyebrows together. "No. Nothing has happened to me. I haven't gone through a divorce or a death or a trauma or..." He trailed off, feeling stupid for no good reason. "Nothing has happened to me."

"Life has happened. It always wounds."

"I'm not wounded."

She didn't argue, and for some reason that bothered him even more.

"I'm not wounded," he repeated, raising his voice slightly—in insistence, not in anger. "Nothing has happened to me."

He thought about Mark, who'd lived through hell on earth.

He thought about Marie, who was ending a marriage to a bastard.

He thought about little Jamal and the other famine victims in Sudan he'd been surrounded by for the past few months.

Nothing had ever happened to him since his parents had died—nothing that could legitimately cause wounds.

They were both silent for a moment, and John was relieved when Cecily's expression changed as if she were moving on from the topic. She smiled at him. "You're the one who keeps feeding that seagull on the side of the building, aren't you?"

John blinked in surprise. "Uh…"

She laughed. "Zeke was complaining about the crumbs."

"He was hungry," John admitted, thinking about that resilient little bird who showed up every morning for the biscuit he crumbled for him.

She reached over and put a light hand on his arm, evidently not concerned about his sweatiness, despite the fact that she was clean and perfectly put together. "You've got a good heart. I like that. I hope you also give it to someone human soon."

John had felt grumpy and unsettled and not particularly worthwhile in the days he'd been here, so he was surprised by the sentiment.

But he couldn't help but think about Betsy as Cecily walked away.

~

After lunch, John was sitting on the patio, reading and wondering if Betsy was going to stop by today—she'd said she would try but it hadn't sounded definite—when someone clapped a hand on his shoulder.

The touch startled him so much he dropped his book in his lap.

"Wow," Mark said with a broad grin. "You're on edge, aren't you? I thought you were supposed to be relaxing."

John jumped to his feet as he processed his brother's presence and reached out to pull Mark into a brief hug. "Why didn't you tell me you were coming?"

"You know me—big on surprises."

John scanned his brother's face and was pleased to see he'd gained more weight in the past few months. He'd been frighteningly skinny when he'd come home a year and a half ago. He still wore a beard—when he'd always been clean-shaven before—but it was neatly trimmed, and he looked healthy and mostly happy.

He was doing better.

A lot better.

Better than John had known he could pray for.

It was only then that John realized Mark wasn't alone. He would have expected his wife, Sophie, to be with him—and he would have been very pleased to see her. But it wasn't Sophie. It was another man—about the same height as Mark, with brown hair and intelligent brown eyes.

"I'm Daniel," the man said, reaching a hand out to him. "Daniel Duncan."

John processed the name and immediately realized who it was. Daniel was the pastor of Mark's church in Willow Park, the small mountain town he lived in.

John tried to hold on to his smile as he shook the other man's hand. "It's nice to meet you."

Daniel laughed—a warm, genuine laugh that was impossible to doubt—and raised his hands in mock surrender. "Don't look at me that way! I promise I wasn't brought along to preach or do counseling sessions. Mark wanted some company, and I've been wanting to check this place out."

John relaxed as he glanced over at his brother's face and realized this was true.

He might feel like an object of sympathy lately—and bristle at the feeling—but there wasn't any underlying agenda to Mark's choice of companion.

Daniel was obviously a friend of Mark's. That was good.

"Sophie couldn't come out too?" he asked.

Mark shook his head. "She has to cover the bookstore this weekend. She told me to say hi, though, and to make sure you were taking it easy."

"You can tell her you found me reading in the middle of the day, and you can't take it easier than that."

"I'll let you guys catch up for a while," Daniel said, glancing toward the door leading into the building. "I want to talk to the director of this place anyway. Her name is Evans?"

"Cecily Evans. Yes. She's probably in her office. She usually is." John watched as Daniel left the patio, and then he turned to Mark. "You didn't have to drive all the way out here."

"It's not that long a drive." Mark sat down and stretched out on the chaise next to John's, so John sat back down too.

"I'm supposed to visit you for a couple of weeks after I'm done here," he said. "If that's all right with you and Sophie. Those are the orders I've been given anyway."

"I know. I'm glad."

John frowned. "Glad I'm going to visit, or glad that someone is giving me obnoxious orders?"

"Both," Mark answered with a chuckle.

"You're enjoying this far too much."

Mark's smile faded slightly, even though John's tone had been light. "Folks were worried about you."

"I know. I keep telling everyone that there was no reason for it. I wasn't on the verge of a breakdown or anything."

"That's not what I heard from Betsy."

John's heart did a weird little jump at hearing her name. "Yeah, well, Betsy... Betsy must have exaggerated some."

"I don't think she did."

"I admit I probably needed a break, but it wasn't as bad as all that. Betsy just worries."

"She doesn't strike me as the kind of person to worry over nothing. She seems pretty level-headed to me."

"She is."

Mark had been looking out at the ocean, but at this he glanced over at John. "Anything going on there?"

John stiffened. "Going on where?"

"With Betsy."

"Why would you think that?"

Mark lifted one shoulder with a clearly suppressed smile. "Oh, no reason."

"We work together."

"That's not an unavoidable obstacle."

"I know, but it's never been like that between us."

"Why not?"

John had no idea how to answer that question because at the moment he had no idea why he and Betsy had never gotten closer.

He wanted to be closer. He couldn't seem to think of anything else since he'd kissed her two days ago.

"She's dating someone else," he said at last when he realized Mark was waiting for an answer.

"What? You're kidding!"

"Why are you surprised? She's gorgeous and smart and sweet and..." When he realized what he was saying, he closed his mouth.

Mark chuckled. "I just always thought you and she would get it together. Who is she dating?"

"Some guy. She just met him earlier this week."

"And they're already dating?"

"Well, they went out last night."

"And how do you feel about that?"

"What does it matter? She can do what she wants."

"And you let a little competition scare you off? That doesn't sound like you."

"What am I supposed to do? Demand that she not see anyone else?"

"Well, that's probably not too smart—not if you want to stay on her good side. But you could try to do something about it yourself."

John remembered his intense feelings as he'd kissed her in the sand. He vividly remembered how his whole body had roared with need and satisfaction, how his heart had started to free-fall.

He wanted more of it. A lot more.

He let out a long breath. "She's kind of pulling away from me."

"Since when?"

"Since this week. I've been noticing it more and more. I don't know if she's even going to visit me today."

"What did you do?"

"Why do you assume I did anything?"

"What did you do?" Mark was frowning thoughtfully.

He'd kissed her. And then felt guilty because he'd lost control so completely. And told her it couldn't happen again.

But it had felt like she'd been pulling away from him even before then. He didn't like it at all, but there didn't seem to be anything he could do about it.

When he didn't respond, Mark went on, "Whatever it is, I'm sure you can fix it. If you want to, I mean."

"Yeah." John closed his eyes against the warmth of the sun. "I'm not even sure what I want."

"So you figure it out. That's what we do."

It sounded so simple, so obvious. But none of this felt simple or obvious to John.

What he wanted felt wrong, felt selfish, felt forbidden. But what he thought he was supposed to do felt barren and cold and hard.

He had absolutely no idea what he should do.

~

Betsy didn't visit on Saturday at all, but they'd made plans to go to church on Sunday morning, and John hoped that hadn't changed.

Maybe she was just giving him time with his brother on Saturday, but John was going to be sorely disappointed if she didn't show up to go to church with him.

He felt naked and helpless without his phone. He couldn't even text or call to verify she was coming. But he got dressed in decent clothes—khaki trousers and a blue dress shirt—and went downstairs at around nine to read and hope someone was going to show up.

Mark definitely would.

He hoped Betsy would too.

Every time he heard a sound, he glanced up at the door to check, and he felt a wave of pleasure when he looked up a half hour later to see Betsy walking into the lobby.

She wore a skirt with a summery top, and her hair was loose again. His body immediately took interest in the length of bare leg he could see and the way her hair brushed against her shoulders.

He was staring so fixedly that he almost failed to notice that Mark had walked in behind her.

"Good morning," she said brightly, smiling like she was glad to see him. "I picked up a straggler."

She was obviously talking about Mark, and John knew he was supposed to make a teasing remark in response. All of them expected it. He even opened his mouth to do it.

But his mind was so filled with Betsy that he couldn't voice any words.

Both Betsy and Mark kept staring at him expectantly.

He felt like an idiot. Like a teenager. What the hell was even wrong with him? He might be out of practice socially, but surely he was capable of making conversation with an attractive woman.

"Hi," he finally managed to say, smiling at her.

Mark's eyes sparkled with amusement. "Were you going to say hello to me too, or no?"

John shook himself off. "Of course. It was a general greeting."

"Right." Mark was obviously still laughing to himself—most likely laughing at John. "Daniel's in the car. He was excited about going to church. He says one of his favorite things about traveling is visiting new churches. Since he's a preacher, he can only visit other churches on the few weekends he has off."

"To each his own, I guess."

Despite their light tone, Betsy's smile faded. "I hope you'll like this church. I grew up in it, but it's grown a lot since I was a member, and it's gotten kind of contemporary, I think."

"That doesn't bother me," Mark said.

Betsy, however, was looking at John, who tried not to make a face. "I'm sure it will be fine."

He'd been to some very fine churches with contemporary worship services.

He'd been to a lot more that were very, very bad.

He and Betsy had been to churches all over the world, and she knew his very strong opinions about their purpose and structure.

Because Betsy was still looking at him questioningly, he repeated, "I'm sure it will be fine. I'll be good. I promise."

Mark snorted, but Betsy smiled—and since that was what he'd been going for, it felt like a victory.

~

Church wasn't great, but it wasn't as bad as he'd feared.

It was the typical, generic contemporary service—a lot of singing of mostly empty words to overly loud musical accompaniment with a couple of prayers and a short, decent sermon.

He tried hard not to be negative, and he found himself focusing on God rather than his natural inclinations to criticize the inane song lyrics, repeated endlessly, and the way the music leader clearly thought he was performing at a concert rather than helping others worship.

The last song, however, went on forever, and the words weren't just superficial. They took lines from the Bible completely out of context. He knew the song was popular. Most of the people around him were clearly into it—raising their hands and closing their eyes. But John couldn't stand it, and the song just wouldn't end.

He was clenching his jaw around his impatience when Betsy leaned over toward him and said into his ear, "Stop criticizing."

He'd been aware of her beside him the whole time, but this was the first time she'd talked to him since the service started. "I didn't say a word."

"You were criticizing in your mind." Because of the volume of the music, she had to speak right into his ear for him to hear her. Her hair brushed against his skin, and he breathed in the light, fresh scent of her.

His body tightened immediately, a response that was so inappropriate in this setting that he gave himself a quick mental lecture.

John was saved from answering by the song finally coming to a close. Then the preacher was praying and giving the benediction, and John let out a relieved sigh.

"You said you were going to be good," Betsy said with a little smile as the congregation started to break up and disperse.

"I was good. I was good almost the whole time."

She giggled, and John experienced a ridiculous swell of pride that he'd made her laugh that way.

"That last song. That was…" Daniel trailed off, evidently remembering that he was supposed to be polite.

In talking to the other man yesterday, John had discovered Daniel was almost as outspoken as he was.

"It was terrible," Betsy whispered, looking a little guilty at the admission.

"Oh good," Mark said in an exaggerated groan. "I thought it was just me missing the point. But was it actually saying that God is only close to us when we feel him? That doesn't sound right at all."

"It's not right," John muttered, still bothered by the implicit lies in the song that so many people sang so earnestly. "At least the other songs were just empty."

"Don't be so judgy. They weren't all empty."

John arched his eyebrows.

"We sang 'Great is Thy Faithfulness.' Surely you don't think that one is empty!" Betsy looked troubled now, rather than amused.

"No. That one's good. Words don't still speak so powerfully to people hundreds of years later unless they're really good. I wish people would remember that when they write worship songs today." He'd gotten into the topic now and had forgotten he was going to prove to Betsy how easygoing and agreeable he could be.

Daniel laughed. "Should we think about how many hymns were written in the past four hundred years that no one knows anymore? I'm sure just as big a percentage were empty or wrong theologically. The good stuff endures. It will endure from what's written today too."

John frowned, mostly because he realized Daniel was right and he wasn't used to being outdone in a conversation.

He didn't like it.

Especially in front of Betsy.

He was good at talking, at thinking, at arguing. It would be nice if Betsy could see and appreciate that.

"If you like the hymn, you could have at least sung along to that one," Betsy murmured, returning to their earlier conversation.

"I did sing."

"You moved your mouth a little. You weren't really singing."

"I'm not much of a singer." They'd been to church together a hundred times. He didn't know why she was bringing this up now when she never had before.

"That doesn't matter. Don't you ever just let yourself go?" Although Mark and Daniel were still part of this conversation, for some reason it felt like John and Betsy were alone.

He shifted from foot to foot. "You mean like all those people with that ridiculous song? That's not worship. That's just working yourself into an emotional state and falsely believing you have to feel that to be close to God."

"I know. I know. That's not what I mean. I mean just…" She trailed off and dropped her eyes.

He reached out without thinking and lifted her chin so he could meet her gaze again. "You mean what?"

"Nothing. Sorry. I was just rambling."

She hadn't been just rambling. She'd been seeing something in him, finding something lacking—and John couldn't stand the thought of it.

He didn't want anything to be lacking in him.

He didn't want Betsy to think he was anything but good.

He could hardly pursue the conversation right now though. Not in the aisle of a church with his brother and Daniel standing with them. So he blew out his impatience and let it go.

He wondered what Betsy wanted him to be that he wasn't.

~

Betsy dropped them all back at the center and left to have lunch with her mother. Daniel walked off alone to call his wife, so Mark and John stood on the front walk and watched Betsy driving off.

John wished she would have stayed the afternoon.

He hoped she wasn't going to see that guy again anytime soon.

He wanted to ask her about it, but he hadn't. He wasn't sure why he was so reticent. It just felt like the questions would reveal too much.

"What?" John finally demanded when he kept feeling his brother giving him looks.

"You're a real idiot sometimes, you know."

"Thanks a lot." Although the context hadn't been clear, John knew exactly what Mark was referring to.

"You are so into her, and you don't even know it."

John didn't bother to deny the statement. What would be the point? He just muttered, "I know now."

Mark's eyes widened slightly. He clearly hadn't expected his brother to admit it. "So what are you going to do about it?"

"What can I do? I'm her boss. Am I supposed to fire her so I can date her?"

"That's ridiculous. You know that's not the only option. You could probably work something out with your supervisors if you wanted. Or you don't have to stay in that job, you know."

John's spine stiffened. "I'm not going to quit!"

"I'm not saying you should. I'm just saying it's an option. But you wouldn't react like that if you hadn't already thought about it."

"I haven't thought about it. I'm not going to quit. My job is important. This is what I do."

"My job before was important too," Mark said softly after a moment's pause. "But I'm not a journalist anymore. Some people might say that what I do now isn't nearly so important, but it's what's right for me right now."

"I know that." John felt that restless wave of guilt again. He hated the feeling. "I'd never think you weren't right to change jobs. But our situations are different. There's no reason for me to quit. I don't want to."

"Fine. So don't. There would still be a way to work things out with Betsy if that's what you wanted. Why won't you even consider the options?"

John didn't have an answer for him.

He'd never considered it before.

He wasn't sure what had changed, but he was definitely considering it now.

SEVEN

That evening, Betsy met Dennis for coffee.

Their date on Friday had gone well—as well as could be expected. She wasn't blown away by him in any way, but she liked him. They might not have a future, but she wanted to prove to herself that her life wasn't on hold.

If she wanted to get married in the future, then she would have to go out with guys.

John might have kissed her on Thursday, but he'd made it clear it wouldn't happen again. She wasn't going to be foolish. She wasn't going to daydream.

She wasn't going to wait around with the futile hope that he'd decide he wanted her for real.

John might not want her, but Dennis did—at least enough to ask her out a second time. They met at a little coffee shop in Avon, and they had a good conversation about their families, pets, and favorite books.

They'd been sitting together for an hour and had fallen into a brief silence, both of them watching the cars drive by on the road outside—half of them pickup trucks with fishing equipment in the back.

"How long do you have off from your job?" Dennis asked.

"A month. It's a kind of sabbatical," she explained, knowing a lot of people raised their eyebrows at the length of a break. "The job we do is hard on you, and even if we have days off, you can't really get away. So you need that time to refresh yourself and recover."

"Of course. I wonder if a month is long enough."

"Sometimes it's not."

"Are you looking forward to going back?"

Betsy hesitated because she wasn't sure how to answer the question honestly. "In some ways I am. In others..."

"How long do you think you'll do it?"

"I don't know. I'm starting to think long-term. It might be time for a change."

"Would you move here?"

"I don't know. I might."

He gave her a little smile. "Is it wrong that I hope you will?"

She blushed slightly and returned his smile. It was impossible not to be pleased that someone appreciated her so simply and openly as Dennis did. Maybe this was what it was like to be with a normal, simple guy.

John was a lot of things, but he definitely wasn't simple.

"How did you get involved in that kind of work to begin with?" Dennis asked after a minute.

"I don't know, really. My college degree was in communications, and I wanted to work with an NGO or a ministry of some kind. So I looked around for positions, and I got a communication job with my organization. I did a few different jobs before I moved to my current team."

"Did you ever think about getting a communication job with some sort of normal company?"

She shook her head. "I really didn't. I just had in mind that I wanted to help people, and this was how I wanted to do it."

"Do you think you could be happy helping people in a little town like this?"

It wasn't a loaded question. She could see he genuinely wanted to know. He was interested—in her, in her history—and he wanted to know her better.

"I..." She cleared her throat. "When I was younger, I didn't think so. I had these lofty goals of helping people in very dramatic ways. I do that now, and I'm glad I do. But I'm starting to think there might be other ways to help people too. I think I could be happy—in a different context. I hope so anyway."

He nodded thoughtfully. "I think a lot of people go through something similar as they get older. I guess it's part of growing up and settling down."

"I suppose." She flashed him a little smile. "Although I don't think I'm that old yet."

He laughed, and Betsy laughed, and she couldn't help but recognize that they got along well.

There was a life here. A life she should probably consider.

A quiet life. Near her mother. In a small town by the ocean. With a man like Dennis.

Far away from John Davenport.

In a way, it would be a relief. Maybe she wouldn't feel this uproar in her heart anymore. Maybe she could find some sort of peace.

~

That night, she was awakened by a call from Nancy, her friend and one of their team members.

Betsy had been asleep, and she was completely disoriented by the unexpected call at almost two in the morning. She managed to grab her phone and connect the call. "Yes?"

"Did I wake you up?" Nancy asked. "I wasn't thinking about the time difference."

"No— Well, yeah. But it's okay. What's going on?"

"Have you checked your email?"

"Not since this morning. What's going on?"

"You'll see an email there from Robert. Jamal died."

Betsy sat up in bed, her heart still throbbing from the shock of the call. But a chill soon overwhelmed her surprise.

Jamal was a little boy the team had helped in Sudan. John had gotten close to him.

John was going to be devastated.

"Oh no," she managed to say.

"I know. It's awful. Anyway, we wanted you to know, but we're thinking that we shouldn't tell John yet. He's going to take it so hard, and then there will be no hope for him really relaxing and getting some rest."

"He'll probably demand to get back to work."

"That's what we thought."

Betsy sighed, her throat aching so painfully she could barely swallow. "Okay. Thanks for telling me. I'll call Chuck in the morning and get his advice about it."

"That's a good idea. Sorry I woke you up."

"It's fine. I'll call you later, okay?"

When she'd hung up, she lay back in bed and stared up at the dark ceiling of her room.

She cried a little bit. For Jamal, whom she had really liked too.

And also for John.

~

The next day, Betsy went to visit John in the middle of the morning, earlier than normal because she felt restless and confused and wanted to get the visit over with since each time she saw him now seemed to work up her emotions even more.

Just one more week. Then he'd be gone, visiting his brother, and something, somehow would be decided.

She wasn't sure whether she would be glad or sad about it.

She'd called Chuck that morning, and he'd agreed they shouldn't tell John about Jamal until these two weeks were over. Betsy knew it was for the best, but it made her feel like she was deceiving him, keeping secrets from him.

She hated to do that.

John wasn't reading on the patio or painting in the studio, and she saw no sign of Zeke, so she wandered around aimlessly, searching.

She finally found John in the pool.

He was swimming laps. She recognized the fine curve of his shoulders and strong lines of his arms as they pulled out of the water with each stroke.

She stood and watched him for a minute until he must have either seen or sensed her presence. He stopped, standing up at the end of the pool, and pulled off the goggles he wore.

"You're here early," he said.

"Yeah. Sorry. I hope it's not too early. It just worked better with my schedule today." That was the truth and didn't reveal anything that couldn't be revealed.

"No, it's fine."

"I didn't know you swam."

"I was on the swim team in high school, but I haven't swum much since." John hauled himself out of the water, and Betsy couldn't help but let her eyes slip down to his body, naked except for the wet swimsuit.

His body was fine. *Very* fine.

She'd never seen a man's body she liked more.

Swallowing hard, she raised her eyes and smiled. "I thought you ran instead."

"I do. I have been. But..."

When he didn't finish the sentence, she was immediately curious. "But what?"

His features twisted with a wry look. "My knees are killing me from running so much on the sand. So I thought I'd swim today instead."

She laughed. It was just like him to be embarrassed about admitting his knees were hurting. He was always trying to be so invincible.

He'd grabbed a towel and was blotting his skin dry. While he was rubbing down his hair, she couldn't help but sneak another look at his broad chest. He had very good pectorals and a deliciously masculine scattering of dark hair. He had dark hair low on his flat belly too, leading down in a thin line beneath the waistband of his suit.

Betsy swallowed again and looked away.

"I'll let you shower and dress if you want," she said, hoping she sounded mostly natural. "I have time."

"Nah, it's fine. No need to waste your time with that." He gestured her toward a table and a couple of chairs with the best view of the ocean, and she had to resign herself to going through this visit with John only half-dressed.

They went to sit down, and she said, "Mark called last night. He and Daniel got back to Willow Park in good time."

"Good. Good. It was nice of him to visit. He didn't have to."

"I'm sure he wanted to. He's your brother. You've gone a lot farther to visit him."

Her words were true. She knew very well that John had flown halfway across the world to see his brother. More than once.

She liked how devoted the brothers were to each other. It made her happy. And not just because it was good to know John had someone who loved him so much.

She just liked to see the closeness. She'd never had any siblings. She often wished she did.

"Did you do anything interesting yesterday evening?" she asked, searching for a topic of easy conversation that wouldn't make her chest ache or stomach flutter.

"Not really. They had a cookout here, so I hung out there for a while. Then I just read. What about you?"

She should have realized asking that question would lead her into this trap, but now she was stuck. She cleared her throat. "I, uh, had coffee with someone."

John's expression changed visibly. "With someone?"

"With Dennis. The dentist."

John had looked friendly earlier—genuinely glad to see her—but now he was almost scowling. "Dennis the dentist. He should put that on his sign."

"Don't be snide."

"Was I being snide?"

"Yes. Kind of. He's a nice guy."

"Evidently, if you've gone out with him twice in three days."

"It's not like that. We're just casual. I'm just starting to get to know him. What's wrong with that?"

"Did I say anything was wrong it?"

"Well, you're acting very grumpy about it. Why shouldn't I go out with someone?"

He was still frowning, and his body looked tense instead of relaxed. "Did I say you shouldn't go out with someone?"

"You don't have to say it when you look so bad-tempered about it. It would be nice if you could be supportive."

"I'll be supportive," he grumbled.

"When are you going to start?"

He obviously made an effort to clear his frown. "I'll start now. So you really like this guy?"

"He's nice. I like him well enough. I still don't know him very well."

"What's his story?"

"What do you mean?"

"I don't know. What's his background? How old is he? Does he have a criminal record?"

She ignored the last question because she knew he wasn't serious. "He's around forty, I think."

"He's too old for you."

She rolled his eyes. "No, he's not. Don't be ridiculous."

"Has he been married before?"

"Yes. He got divorced a couple of years ago."

"What happened there?"

She supposed it was natural for him to curious, but it felt more like an interrogation, and she was annoyed by it. "How is that your business?"

"I sure hope it's your business."

"His wife left him for another man. Happy now? I thought you were going to be supportive."

He cleared his expression again. "I am. Sorry. I'm not good at being nice."

She had to laugh at this. "Yes, you are. Your first instinct is to be nice. It's only when you're feeling useless that you start being rude like this. And we keep telling you it's all right for you to take a break every now and then. It doesn't mean you're useless."

She hadn't intended to say so much, but she didn't regret the words.

She wanted him to know that.

She wanted him to believe it.

And she really didn't know if he did.

"I've been feeling pretty useless lately," he admitted gruffly, leaning back in his chair, confirming her thoughts.

"I know you have." Her voice was a lot gentler than before. She couldn't hold herself back, so she reached over and put a hand on his arm. "But I'm telling you that you're not. You don't have to work to be useful. And you don't have to be useful to be of value. Maybe we like having you around just for yourself."

He met her eyes, something strangely questioning, tentative in his expression. "Do you?"

"Of course we do."

"Do you?"

Her breath hitched in her throat. "I do."

When she realized what she'd said—and what it implied—she felt a stab of fear and pulled her hand away.

111

She didn't want to stop touching him, but she needed to. She couldn't let herself fall into this emotional trap.

John might be unusually needy lately, but he'd made it clear he didn't want a relationship with her. She couldn't let herself hope he would.

Not again.

He must have shook himself off internally too because he straightened up and looked away from her. "So are you going to see Dennis the dentist again?"

She frowned, her stomach dropping in disappointment at his dry tone although she knew it was for the best. "I don't know. I might. And I'll keep waiting for you to be supportive about it."

All he said to that was, "Yeah."

~

John was walking her back to the lobby a few minutes later when Betsy heard a loud squawking from the top of the fence surrounding the pool and patio.

She blinked up into the sun and saw a small seagull, perched up there as if he owned the place. The bird kept squawking in that abrasive way seagulls had.

"What's your problem?" she asked the bird. She'd always liked animals—all animals—and she saw nothing strange about talking to them.

"He's probably hungry."

"Why would he think we'd have food for him?"

When John didn't answer, Betsy peered up at his face and saw an expression that was almost guilty.

She gasped. "Have you been feeding him?"

"Just a little." He slanted her an adorably sheepish look.

"How do you know it's this one?"

"Oh, I know. He comes every morning for his biscuit. He has a real attitude about it now."

"You give him a whole biscuit?"

"Not a whole one. I crumble up a piece of one for him. He was real pitiful on the first day, pecking at a hard old fry. I felt bad for him."

Betsy was overwhelmed with the strangest feeling—a mixture of amusement and understanding and fondness.

And something even deeper. A lot deeper.

"It's okay," he said with a twitch of his lips. "You can laugh if you want."

"I don't want to laugh." She did giggle though, and then to her horror it turned into almost a sob.

There was absolutely no reason to be so emotional about something so little, but she was.

John was always picking up strays. It was what he did.

He wanted so much to take care of anything and anyone that might need him.

Even this little bird with an attitude.

It was one of the things she loved about him.

He cared about Jamal so much and still didn't know the boy was dead.

She tried to control herself and pretend she was just laughing, but John seemed to know the difference.

Without saying anything, he wrapped an arm around her and pulled her into a hug.

She burrowed against him, taking comfort in his warmth, in his heart.

But for only a minute. Soon she made herself pull away.

"You better go get him a snack," she said, feeling better at the release of emotional tension. A little embarrassed but better. "He obviously didn't get enough biscuit this morning."

"He's obviously a spoiled ingrate who doesn't deserve anything better."

John's voice was dry, but Betsy knew better. As they were walking through the lobby, she said, "You're going to go find him something as soon as I leave, aren't you?"

"Of course not," John muttered. "He's a bird. He'll have to find his own food."

Both of them knew it wasn't true.

EIGHT

On Tuesday morning, John woke up later than usual.

In fact, he blinked several times at the clock next to this bed, trying to figure out what day it was and whether it was morning or evening. He felt the same way he used to as a kid when he'd taken a long nap and then woken up to have absolutely no idea what was going on.

He never slept past seven, and the clock was right now outrageously claiming it was 8:05.

After staring and rubbing his face a few times, he finally came to the conclusion he'd slept in.

He wasn't on a schedule here, so it didn't matter. But he still felt strange and almost guilty as he dressed. He didn't shower because he was going to swim right after breakfast. He wanted to be finished if Betsy decided come visit him early again, the way she had yesterday. Because he'd just gotten out of the pool, they hadn't been able to do anything but talk.

He wanted her to stay longer today, so he was going to be showered and dressed when she arrived.

When he went down to breakfast, he felt like people were looking at him, wondering why he'd slept in so late. It was ridiculous, of course. No one probably even noticed. But he couldn't seem to shake that feeling of not doing, being what he was supposed to do and be.

Breakfast passed as usual, and the little seagull was waiting on the fence for his morning biscuit as John went out to crumble it on the ground for him.

He had a little pang of regret about how disappointed the bird would be next week when there was no biscuit left for him to eat.

Then he swam for an hour. His knees were feeling better, but swimming was a lot easier on his body than running, and there was no reason to kill himself just to exercise.

At nine forty-five, he headed back downstairs, dressed and ready for Betsy to arrive.

He felt kind of like an idiot—because there was no reason to assume she'd come in the morning today. Every day except yesterday, she'd come in the middle of the day or later.

He might be sitting around for hours this morning waiting for her.

He didn't have anything else to do though. He was on his third book of the paperbacks Betsy had brought him, and he had half of it left to read. He sat in his normal chaise on the patio and flipped through the pages to find the spot he'd left off on.

He wondered what Betsy was doing at the moment.

Hopefully not talking on the phone with Dennis the dentist.

He rolled his eyes at the thought of him.

It wasn't kind. It wasn't generous. It wasn't in the spirit of Christian charity.

But he just didn't like that guy.

At all.

It didn't matter that he'd never met him.

He'd been reading for about a half hour when he looked up expectantly at a presence beside him. His heart had sped up automatically, and his breath caught in his throat as he thought he would see Betsy beside him.

It wasn't Betsy. It was a woman he didn't know. She wasn't paying any attention to him. She'd clearly sat down right here just to work on her phone. Her entire focus was on whatever she was tapping on the screen.

He watched her for a moment, registering a ludicrous amount of disappointment that it wasn't Betsy.

Then he realized something else that was strange.

She had a phone. Here.

He must have been staring too obviously because she looked over at him after a moment. She was fairly young and quite attractive in that very modern, fashionable way he'd noticed in a lot of women in their twenties and thirties. Her hair was a very light blond, and her tailored trousers and heels looked expensive. So did the big leather bag she'd laid down beside her.

He noticed all this in just a few seconds. Then he said, "How'd you sneak that in here?"

She frowned at him in confusion for a minute—or maybe she just didn't want him to bother her. Then her face relaxed. "The phone, you mean? I'm not staying here. Just visiting."

"Oh. Okay."

He was surprised Zeke allowed her to have it even for a visit, but he didn't question her claim.

"My partner wants us to use this place for a company retreat, so I'm just here checking it out." After a moment, she added, "My business partner."

"It is a nice place," he said—out of basic integrity. He might have been annoyed about having his phone taken away, but he wasn't going to complain about it to a stranger. Not when everyone here had been good to him. "It would be good for a company retreat."

Her little nose wrinkled. "Maybe. So they really don't let you have a phone?"

He shook his head.

"And you're okay with someone taking it from you?"

"I didn't really have a choice. What would I do? Get in a fistfight over my phone?"

"I would." Her voice was dry, and her eyes were intelligent. He recognized that most men must find her incredibly attractive.

It wasn't her fault he kept comparing her to Betsy.

"Do you want to borrow mine for a minute?" she asked, reaching the phone out toward him. "You must feel completely out of touch with the world."

He did.

He really did.

He didn't like the feeling.

But he shook his head. "Thanks though."

"I guess that's why that weird guy in the purple shirt kept glaring at me. Because of the phone."

John chuckled. "I think he glares at everyone, whether you have a phone or not."

"What's his deal anyway?"

"I haven't figured that out yet."

"I'm Vivian, by the way."

He held out his hand to her, smiling. "John."

"Viv!" The voice was male and new. John had never heard it before. He looked over his shoulder to see a man coming out of the lobby. He looked about John's age, and he wore glasses and had an overall rumpled look to him. He was frowning.

"I'm here," she said without turning to look at the approaching man. "No need to shout."

"If you're done flirting with strangers, we've got some other stuff to look at."

This must be her business partner. It wasn't a difficult guess to make.

"No need to be rude about it. Anyway, I wasn't flirting." She turned to John. "Was I flirting?"

John didn't know either of these people, but he felt more loyalty to Vivian than to this other man. He said, "She wasn't flirting."

"Uh-huh," the man said wryly. "Let's go."

Vivian shook her head and gave John one last significant look. "See what I have to put up with? He doesn't even seem to care that I'm the senior partner."

"Viv," the man said impatiently.

John chuckled at Vivian's eye-roll as she and the man walked down toward the pool.

He was still watching them idly when a voice came from over his shoulder. "Who was that?"

He gave a dramatic and rather embarrassing jerk.

Betsy.

She was here, and he hadn't even realized it.

Excitement vied with confusion inside him as he tried to process her presence and how delectable she looked in a pink top and tan capris with her hair hanging down over her shoulders again.

"Well?" she prompted after a minute.

He remembered then that she'd asked him a question. "Who was who?"

"That woman you were talking to."

"Oh, I don't know. She just sat down."

Betsy frowned. "You seemed very friendly to be strangers."

John's mouth fell open slightly at her disapproving tone. "I was just talking to her," he said. "She had a phone, and I was asking her about it. What's the problem?"

"There is no problem. Why would there be a problem? I was just asking."

It was only then that John realized Betsy was reacting exactly the way he'd reacted when she mentioned Dennis the dentist.

She was acting jealous.

Jealous.

About *him*.

Pleasure and excitement tightened in his chest at the realization.

She'd never acted jealous around him before. Maybe she wasn't as interested in the dentist as he'd feared.

"I talked to her for about five minutes. She and her partner are looking at this place for a retreat."

"Oh."

"I just met her."

"That's what you said."

"And I meant it."

"Okay."

"Okay."

He wanted to smile—because he was suddenly happy—but he didn't want her to think he was laughing at her. She looked adorably flustered. Her eyes were lowered, and her hair was hanging down to partially block her face.

He wanted to see her expression, so he reached out to push her hair back behind her shoulder.

She raised her eyes with an audible breath, and they stared at each other for a moment.

He wondered what she would do if he just leaned over and kissed her.

He wanted to so much his eyes clouded over slightly and his whole body got hot.

But the problem wasn't what she would do if that happened. The problem was what *he* would do.

If he let himself kiss her, he wouldn't be able to stop.

Her cheeks flushed pink, and she looked away from him.

He realized he had better start acting normal, or they couldn't even be friends. He cleared his throat. "You're here early again today."

"Yeah. I can come in the afternoon if that works better for you."

"No. No. Any time is great. What else do I have to do?"

She was looking at him again, and she seemed more like herself. Her eyes were observant. "You don't look as annoyed with the world as you did last week. You must not be having a terrible time here."

"I'm not. I'm really not. I even slept well last night and didn't wake up until after eight."

"Really?" Her face brightened at this piece of news. "That's great. So you don't mind it too much?"

"It's okay. I understand the purpose in it. I wouldn't want to do it for long though. It's not even the lack of phone and computer. It's strange, not being able to go out and do something on my own."

"Where do you want to go?"

"Nowhere in particular. It's just not being able to do it that's the issue."

She nodded slowly, like she was trying to understand. "We can go do something if you want to get out. You're not trapped here, you know."

"That would be great. Where do you want to go?"

"I don't have anywhere in mind, but we could do something." Her expression changed in a way he recognized. She'd obviously just come up with an idea. "I know."

"Why do I get the feeling I'm not going to like this plan?"

She giggled. "You'll like it just fine. We'll get to go out and about for a while."

"And do what exactly?"

"My mom asked me to find her a new hat."

John's eyes widened. "What?"

"A new hat. For my mom."

"What kind of hat?"

"A hat with a big brim to keep the sun off her face when she's in the garden. Hers is nearly in tatters."

"You want me to go shopping with you to find your mom a hat?"

"She asked me to."

"Did she ask me to go with you?"

"No, of course not. That would be strange. But you wanted something to do, didn't you?"

John was having trouble holding back his amusement at Betsy's sparkling eyes and twitching mouth. But he managed a stony look. "Shopping for hats wasn't what I had in mind."

"Don't grumble. You'll love it."

~

As it turned out, John did love it.

It didn't really matter that they were looking at hats at a number of tacky beach shops—which seemed to be the extent of shopping locales in the area. It didn't matter that Betsy didn't like any of the very reasonable options of hats he showed her, and so the shopping lasted longer than it should have.

And it didn't matter that John had never liked to shop and always ended up grabbing something easy because anything else left him restless and impatient.

It was really nice to have a change of scenery for a while. And Betsy was in a laughing, teasing mood, so it was impossible for him not to keep smiling and laughing himself.

He couldn't remember the last time he'd had such a good time.

They were on their fourth store, and he was fake grumbling that she had to find a hat here or he would declare the quest a lost cause and her mother would go hatless. Then Betsy got the idea that he needed a hat himself because he had gotten too much sun over the past week. So she kept putting different hats on his head and rippling with laughter at the result.

He enjoyed her laughing so much that he hammed it up for her benefit.

She finally decided on a hat for her mother, and she insisted on buying one of the less offensive hats for him as well. John didn't have the will to argue, even when she put it on his head as they left the shop.

"Did you want to get something to eat?" he asked, realizing he was hungry and it was lunchtime.

"Oh." She glanced at her watch, evidently as surprised by the time as he'd been.

"If you have something else to do, that's fine." His stomach churned slightly at the idea that the other thing she needed to be doing was meeting Dennis.

"I don't have anything else. We can definitely have lunch if you want. There's a good place just down the road, if you don't mind hole-in-the-wall ambience."

"Sounds like my kind of place."

The restaurant turned out to be a basic beach hangout, but the seafood was fresh and the service was good. He and Betsy sat at a table on the deck outside, and he wasn't in any hurry for the lunch to end.

They faded into silence after laughing at the elaborate backstory John had made up for one of the more unsavory fellow patrons, who'd clearly been sitting at the bar inside for more than an hour, even though it was barely after noon.

John kept shooting surreptitious looks at Betsy, wondering what she was thinking, wondering if she was enjoying today as much as he was.

She caught him during one of his looks and smiled at him shyly.

He smiled back, and they sat and gazed at each other for a minute.

Then she gave a little jerk and looked away.

He wondered what she was thinking, why she broke the gaze so abruptly. Like she wasn't supposed to be looking at him that way.

He didn't know why not.

He was sometimes grumpy and occasionally unreasonable, but he wasn't a bad guy over all.

"This feels so far away," she said at last in a slightly wistful voice.

"What does?"

"This does. Being here. It's like you said the other day. It just feels so far away from... from the rest of life."

It did. He knew it did. It was the only reason he was indulging these feelings that he normally would be bundling into a tight ball and hiding away somewhere.

"Yeah," he murmured.

"Do you think it will all go back to... to the way it was before—when we get back to work?"

"I... I don't know."

"Me either." Her face was sobered now—for the first time since he'd seen her first thing this morning.

He didn't like the change in expression. He didn't like that something in her thoughts had upset her. He reached out and covered her hand with his on the table.

Her eyes flew up to his face. She was obviously surprised by the gesture.

He didn't care. He adjusted his fingers so he was taking her hand in his. Her hand was a lot smaller than his. And cooler. He held it gently.

Her cheeks grew pink again, and she smiled, a little fluttery. She didn't say anything.

He didn't either.

His blood was pulsing in his veins now—not with physical desire so much as emotional pleasure. He couldn't remember ever feeling like this before, but he didn't want to let go of Betsy's hand.

So he didn't.

He held it as they finished their drinks, and then he reached for it again as they were leaving.

She didn't pull her hand away.

Maybe it was young and sappy—silly and not the kind of man John had always imagined himself—but he didn't care. He almost never felt this way, and he didn't want it to go away.

~

Later that afternoon, after Betsy left, John took a walk on the beach.

Thinking of Betsy, he even took off his shoes and walked barefoot through the surf, feeling the sand between his toes and cool water lap around his ankles.

He wanted to keep thinking about Betsy—about how happy he'd been with her lately—but it felt like there was a gathering wave in the back of his mind, ready to crash at any moment.

He didn't quite know what the threatening wave was, but it got stronger every time he thought of his work, of his unread email, of Jamal. And even in his downtime, it always felt like he was mentally trying to hold all that back before it buried him.

If all that was waiting to crash into him the moment he left this place, then he might as well enjoy his time here while he could.

He gazed out at the water and noticed a small speedboat zooming over the waves in the distance.

He would like to be out on a boat.

Maybe Betsy would go with him.

He wondered if there was a boat around here he could use.

He would ask Zeke or Cecily when he got back to the center.

NINE

The next morning, Betsy was taking her mother to the grocery store and trying not to think about John.

She was completely unsuccessful.

It felt like her whole being was buzzing with excitement—every breath she took and sight she saw somehow more vivid and delightful than usual. She wasn't foolish enough to not know why.

She wanted to be with John right now. She wanted him to hold her hand the way he had the day before.

She wanted him to do even more.

Maybe he would.

For the first time, she had legitimate hope, and it was absolutely intoxicating.

She didn't want to be the kind of selfish, ungrateful daughter who would resent spending time with her mother because she'd rather be with her man, so she kept trying to calm down and focus on the grocery shopping trip.

She must have failed because, as they were parking in the small lot, her mother asked out of the blue, "This isn't about Dennis, is it?"

"What?"

"This mood... It isn't about Dennis, is it?"

"I'm not in any kind of mood." Maybe if she said the words, they would become true.

They didn't. Betsy was definitely in a mood today. Every time she thought about John, she felt like hugging herself.

Her mother gave her a familiar, narrow-eyed look. "Is there something going on with John that I should know about?"

"N-no." Okay, that didn't sound too convincing.

"Elizabeth."

"I'm just in a good mood, is all."

"This is more than a mood. I thought you were going to be careful and get some distance."

"I was. I am. But he's... Something has changed. I don't think I'm being stupid." She'd put the car into the park, unhooked her seat belt, and turned to face her mother.

"Has he said something?"

"N-no. But... I'm really not an idiot. I know something has changed. He's been... giving me real signs."

"You said he was going through some things right now."

"He is." Betsy didn't like where this was going. It was bringing down her giddy mood.

"Isn't it possible that those signs and changes are a result of whatever he's going through and not because he's made a conscious, informed decision to pursue a relationship with you?"

Betsy turned away, her stomach twisting slightly. "Sure. It's possible. But why won't you believe that he could... he could actually fall for me. I know I'm not exactly romance material, but—"

"Betsy, stop!" her mother interrupted, her expression changing. "You're beautiful and smart and loving, and any man would be thanking God night and day if you chose him. I'm not saying he wouldn't."

"Then why are you so discouraging about this? I'm really not imagining things with John."

She remembered how it had felt yesterday when he'd reached over and taken her hand. She could see his expression very clearly.

It meant something. She knew it did.

She wasn't making it up.

"I'm not trying to be discouraging." Her mother suddenly looked older and very tired. "I'm sorry if it's coming across that way. I... I just want you to be smart."

"Can't I be smart and hopeful at the same time?"

"Maybe you can. I don't know. But it's been my experience that, if a man doesn't actually say something, then there's not much room for real hope. I just want you to protect your heart."

Betsy thought about that, and her stomach dropped a little more. Maybe her mother was right. Maybe whatever was happening with John wasn't built on a firm enough foundation for her to put her trust in.

"My own experiences might have clouded my judgment," her mother added in a different tone.

Betsy took a sharp breath. "Your own experiences?"

"With your father. All the signs were there too. He was acting like he loved me. I let my feelings lead me to bad decisions—because I kept assuming his actions were speaking louder than words and that he meant things he hadn't said. I assumed he loved me and would marry me because that was the way he was acting. I was wrong. And I had to live with the devastation."

"My father was a... a jerk." She reworded her initial thoughts out of respect for her mother's sensitivities. "He was selfish and took advantage of you. John isn't like that."

"I know your John is different. I know he's a good man. But I've told you before. Even good men will sometimes unintentionally play with our hearts."

Betsy knew this was true. But it didn't feel true with John.

She didn't want it to be true.

She wanted to just revel in the fact that a man finally, *finally* wanted her. For real.

She swallowed hard. "I know. I'm trying to be careful. But I don't want to be so careful that I... I discourage him."

"A strong man who knows what he wants isn't going to be discouraged because you're not rushing into things."

"I know."

"Do you?"

"Yes. I do."

"Good."

Betsy didn't think it was good. The whole conversation had cast a pall on her bright mood. And it made her question everything that had happened over the past few days.

She didn't like it to be questioned.

At all.

~

Four hours later, Betsy was out on a boat with John.

He'd been painting when she arrived, and when she'd seen the boat on his canvas, she'd said it was too bad there wasn't a boat they could use.

John had said they did have a boat here at Balm in Gilead. He'd talked to Zeke about it the day before. He could take her out if she wanted.

So here they were—sitting on a small motorboat, enjoying a very sunny day on the water.

Betsy loved it.

All her doubts about this relationship disappeared as soon as she'd seen John. He'd smiled at her in that particular way—warm, intimate, almost sweet—and she'd known she wasn't letting her heart rule her head.

There was something here, and it was real. She wasn't making it up in some sort of childish daydream.

She glanced over at him as he was fiddling with the motor. They'd come out far enough to be alone on the water, and then he'd turned off the engine. The boat was rocking, but the waves weren't particularly rough, so the motion was soothing rather than dramatic.

John wore sunglasses, and he looked gorgeous and masculine in his casual clothes. His skin was a lot tanner than it had been last week, and there was a slight shadow of bristles on his jaw, even though she knew he had shaved that morning.

And Betsy had a sudden, overwhelming realization. She couldn't believe that this man would ever want to be with her. Not for real. Not for good. He was so handsome and so smart and so good in every way.

He was just hanging out here with her. That must be all it was.

If he were really choosing, he would choose someone other than her.

The knowledge burned in her throat, affecting her so much she had to turn away and breathe deeply.

She wasn't as insecure as she'd been as a girl, but some things never fully went away. And she couldn't imagine—she just couldn't imagine—that a man like John would ever really want someone as plain and unexciting as her.

Basic Betsy. It was who she'd always been.

"What's the matter?" he asked from behind her.

Damn it. "Nothing," she said, turning back around with a smile. "I was just looking around."

He didn't appear to believe her. His brows were pulled together. "Did something upset you?"

Of course it had upset her. Her mother had been right all along. "No. Why would you think that?"

"You just looked..." He reached out to take off her sunglasses so he could see her eyes. Then he picked up one of her hands, rubbing the palm gently with his thumb. "Maybe I was imagining it, but it looked like something had hurt you. I'm not okay with that. I'm not okay with anything hurting you."

So there her heart went all into flutters again. She gave him a slightly trembly smile. "Nothing is hurting me."

"Good. Because I'm not going to let it."

They sat for a minute, holding hands as the sun beat down on them, and Betsy told herself her fears were just a lingering result of her old insecurities.

She was a worthwhile, valuable person—in God's eyes and in the eyes of the world. There was no reason a man couldn't fall in love with her. Just because no one ever had, didn't mean no one ever would.

She wasn't going to let her old fears hold her back anymore.

She smiled at him and used her free hand to take off his sunglasses, the way he had hers. "It's only fair," she said at his questioning look. "I want to see your eyes too."

His smile warmed, and her whole body started to pulse.

He didn't lean over and kiss her, but he didn't need to. They sat holding hands for a long time, and they didn't talk.

She just let herself enjoy the moment, enjoy John's presence, enjoy the beauty and warmth of creation.

There weren't always moments of peace and joy like this in her life, and she wanted to bask in it for as long as she could.

"It's like that hymn," John murmured after several minutes of silence. He was still holding her hand, occasionally stroking her palm in a way that felt special, tender.

"What hymn?"

"Morning by morning new mercies I see."

"Yes." It was like he had read her mind, and it confirmed how perfectly in sync they were. "It's exactly like that." She gave him a teasing smile. "We should sing it."

He arched his eyebrows dryly. "You can sing it for me. You've got a good voice."

"I'll only sing it if you sing it too, but you have to really sing—not just move your lips and occasionally make a little noise."

He curled his mouth at her, but she just laughed. "I'm serious. You have to really sing. I want to see if you really know how to do it."

"I know how to sing. Not well, but..."

"I don't mean knowing how to sing. I mean I want to see if you know how to really let yourself go, surrender to the joy God gives you—not always try to control yourself all the time. I want to see if you can... you can relinquish. Be free."

She hadn't really intended to say all that, but the words embodied so much of what she'd been thinking about him for the past week, all the ways he always held himself back from genuinely enjoying—living—life.

He gazed at her silently for a moment.

She didn't know what to say or what to do, so she just started singing the first verse of "Great is Thy Faithfulness."

She was pleased and relieved and washed with a wave of joy when John started to sing it too.

He really didn't have a bad voice at all. He stayed on key, and he had a pleasant resonance to his deep voice. They sang together well, but soon she forgot about how she sounded.

She thought about the words, about their meaning, about unchanging faithfulness in her life—even when everything else changed.

She teared up a little on the second verse, really feeling what it meant in joining with all nature in testifying to God's nature on this beautiful day, surrounded by sky and ocean and sunshine.

John was really singing—in a way he never did in church. She'd teased him about never really letting himself go, but there was real truth in that observation. He was always so afraid of relinquishing control that he couldn't let loose his heart.

He was now though, and it just added to her joy of the moment.

On the third verse, John stopped singing.

She glanced over at him and saw something happening on his face. It was tight with emotion, and he was staring blindly out at the water.

She kept singing because she didn't know what else to do. She knew he was dealing with something—something that wasn't about her.

Whatever he was dealing with was spiritual and intense and private, so she didn't ask about it or expect him to share.

It went on a long time. When she finished the hymn, she started singing it again from the beginning, and John sat beside her the whole time, holding her hand tighter and tighter, lost in his own intense reflections.

He was praying or thinking or struggling with emotion—or all of them at once.

It felt important, so she prayed for him silently.

When she finished the hymn the second time, she fell into quiet. Her hand was actually hurting now—he was gripping it so hard.

She was breathing in fast little pants, anxious and hopeful and confused and frightened all at once. Her skin was flushed, and she tried to show her support through her grip on John's hand since it was the only way she had at the moment to show it.

It was several more minutes before John finally turned to look at her. His voice was hoarse when he said, "I've spent my whole life trying to be good. Trying not to let God or anyone else down. I've been so focused on it that I'm not sure I even know how to worship... how to love."

"That's not true," she said, rising immediately to his defense. "You do know how to love."

He lifted one of his shoulders in a slight shrug. "Maybe. I don't know. But I don't want to be like that. I don't think God wants me to—or expects me to."

"He doesn't." It was exactly what she'd suspected, hoped, he'd been reflecting on.

"I know."

She waited for him to say more, but he didn't. He'd loosened his grip on her hand but hadn't let it go yet.

Finally he cleared his throat. "I was... I had snuck out at night and gone to a party I wasn't supposed to the night my parents were killed. I got drunk and was in bad shape, so one of my buddies called them. They were out to dinner, but they left and were coming to get me. Another car ran a... a stoplight. They were both killed instantly."

Mark had alluded to it but had not told her any of the details. She was horrified and heartbroken and full of understanding she hadn't had before. It filled in the missing pieces of her picture of John—why he was so afraid of enjoying himself and not doing what he was supposed to do. "That wasn't your fault, John. You can't possibly think it was your fault."

"I know."

"It doesn't mean you're not allowed to have fun and enjoy life. God doesn't want your empty duty. He wants your love."

"I know."

"John..." She wasn't sure what she wanted to say, so she just trailed off.

He met her eyes with a little smile. "I'm going through some real soul-searching over here, and all you can say is my name? I'm waiting for some more words of wisdom."

She dissolved into giggles, relieved and even more emotional at his fond, teasing tone and the breaking of the tension. She finally pulled her hand away from his but only to reach around him with both arms and give him a hug.

He wrapped his arms around her too, pulling her against him tightly.

They hugged silently for a minute, and Betsy couldn't remember ever feeling so close to another person.

She didn't want it to end.

Maybe it wouldn't.

Maybe she would be allowed to be close to John like this for the rest of her life.

After all, it hadn't happened before, but it wasn't impossible.

~

They returned to the dock at Balm in Gilead not long after. It felt like everything that needed to happen had happened, and Betsy was overwhelmed with happiness and tenderness and hope.

So much hope.

She felt strangely shy as John helped her out of the boat. She could barely bring herself to look him in the eye.

"Betsy," he murmured, his gentle tone causing her to raise her eyes to his face. His eyes were just as tender as his voice. "Sweetheart."

He'd never called her that before. He usually called her just Bets.

The word felt like more than just an endearment.

It felt like he really meant it.

"Do you have to leave now?" he asked.

Her heart made several little leaps. "I told my mom I'd be back for dinner. She's making something."

"Just your mom?"

She realized what he was asking, what it meant. "Yes. Just my mom."

"No one else?"

"No one else." She had a call to return to Dennis, but at the moment it was the last thing she wanted to do.

He nodded, evidently pleased by this piece of news. "Maybe you could come back after dinner."

She swallowed. "Maybe."

"Will you?" His eyes were soft and questioning and so incredibly beautiful.

Everything she wanted.

"Okay. I will."

He smiled then, and she smiled back, and he leaned down to press his lips very gently against hers.

It was such a gentle little kiss—barely a brush of his mouth—but it made her mind and heart and body explode with feeling just the same.

"Good," he murmured, his breath wafting against her lightly. "I'm glad. Things don't feel right in the world without you."

It was as close as he'd come to a declaration of feeling, and it gave Betsy even more hope.

He wasn't just holding her hand.

He wasn't just kissing her.

He'd actually said that he wanted to spend time with her, that it was important to him that she was around.

He wasn't just playing around with her. He wasn't taking advantage of her.

This meant something to him—maybe as much as it meant to her.

She could trust him. She always had.

He wasn't going to break her heart.

He wasn't that kind of man.

TEN

Two days later, John was wondering when Betsy would arrive this morning.

Only a couple more days, and his two weeks at Balm in Gilead would be over.

In a way he was glad since he still felt uncomfortably stranded and helpless without a phone or car. But he would miss it here. He couldn't remember feeling so rested, so free—not since he was a boy, before his parents had died, had he felt like this.

Sometimes it felt like payback was still lurking in that threatening wave, like he couldn't let himself go so much without terrible consequences. He was trying to talk himself out of that kind of irrationality though.

He was happy. Betsy was happy too.

Surely there wasn't anything wrong with this. Surely it wouldn't all end as soon as he stepped outside these doors.

He looked up when someone came over to sit down on the chair next to him on the patio. Since he'd swum this morning and had just come down after showering and dressing, he hadn't taken his normal chaise. Betsy would be here any minute.

Cecily smiled at him. "Waiting for Betsy?"

"Yes. She's supposed to be here soon."

"It looks like things are going well there." Cecily's face was warm and friendly, despite the careful wording of her statement.

Things were going well. Ever since that afternoon on the boat, when he'd come to that unexpected spiritual epiphany, they'd been practically inseparable. He hadn't said anything yet, but it was clear to both of them that their relationship had changed.

It was new and exciting and breathtaking... and occasionally terrifying. John was still waiting to get a handle on his new feelings before he made anything definite.

But things were definitely going well.

When he failed to answer Cecily's question, she arched her eyebrows.

"Oh, yeah," he said quickly. "I guess it is."

"I usually recommend that people don't begin or deepen relationships while they're staying here." She was speaking lightly and still smiling—it didn't look like she was trying to give him an underlying message. "People staying here are often letting go of old restraints or trying to be someone new, so it's not always a good idea to add romance into the mix since what works here doesn't always translate into the rest of their lives. But you and Betsy have known each other for a long time. You seem to have a real foundation, so I don't worry about that with you two. I'm happy for you both." She reached over to pat his forearm companionably before she got up. "It's nice to see her so happy."

John watched as she walked away, hit strangely by her words.

Betsy *was* happy. And he was the reason for it—at least part of the reason.

That made him responsible for it.

And what if Cecily was right about his time here? Maybe what he was feeling here, now, wouldn't last once he got back to the real world. He could hardly remember the real world at the moment. Everything seemed to be sunshine and salty breezes and the touch of Betsy's hand.

But it wasn't.

There was famine in the real world. And war. And car accidents. And heartbreak around every corner.

Maybe, when he left this place, he would break Betsy's heart.

Maybe she would break his.

He hadn't even checked his email in days. He wondered how Jamal was doing.

With a painful wave of guilt, he realized he hadn't even thought about Jamal in a couple of days.

He was still trying to come to grips with this reality when a voice broke through his grim reflections. "John? What's the matter?"

He jerked and blinked up at Betsy's lovely, worried face. "Nothing. Nothing."

She frowned. "Well, something's wrong."

"I was just thinking about Jamal, wondering how he's doing."

Her features twisted briefly. "Oh."

He'd upset her now. He could see that very clearly. He stood up and pulled her into a soft hug.

She relaxed against him, and her soft body felt better against him than anything he could remember.

"You feel good," he murmured against her hair.

She laughed softly but didn't pull away. "And you just took a shower. You smell like soap."

"Is that a problem?"

"Not at all." She finally drew back and smiled up at him, looking bright and amused. "Far better than many alternatives."

"Nice." He gave her the offended look he knew she was expecting and then glanced toward the beach. "Do you want to walk?"

"Sure."

They walked down to the wet sand and then started south, and John reached out for her hand.

"I can't believe you only have two more days here," she said after a minute.

"I know. The two weeks seemed to last forever and disappear overnight, if both those things are possible."

"It feels that way for me too."

She smiled over at him, and for a moment he couldn't breathe over how beautiful she looked in the sunshine, how much he wanted to always be with her, the way he would feel if she were no longer in his life.

He had no idea he was capable of feeling this way.

He wasn't used to letting emotion have so much power over him. He didn't know how to deal with it.

"I'm going to miss you when you go to visit Mark for two weeks," she added.

John swallowed. He was going to miss her too. So much so that he wondered if things would change once he was gone from here, once they were separated. "It's just two weeks," he said since he knew she was waiting for a response.

"I know." She cleared her throat. Took a strange little breath. "Maybe we should talk about what happens afterward."

His stomach did a weird twisting thing. He had a vision in his mind of what might happen afterward, but it would mean that everything had changed.

His whole life. His life's purpose. Everything.

He'd never believed himself to be the kind of person to throw away a valuable career—one that genuinely helped others—in order to indulge in private desires.

"John?" she prompted. "I'm not pushing or anything. But our job positions are... are an issue... with this. We do eventually need to talk."

He'd made her uncomfortable, worried, and he hated himself for doing it. He managed to say, "I know. We will. I'm still... working through things in my mind."

"Okay," she said lightly. "But just so you know, we can work through them together."

He wanted to do that so much it terrified him.

Who was this person he was turning into?

"You're stewing," she said after a moment.

"No, I'm not."

"Yes, you are. I haven't seen you stewing like this in a few days. What's the matter?"

He shook his head and reached to take her hand. "Nothing. Nothing, really. I'm just trying to sort things out. I promise it's nothing important."

He felt better because she visibly relaxed and smiled at him.

Then he wondered why it felt like she was the most important person in the world.

That shouldn't be right. Should it?

∼

They walked for nearly an hour, and then he bought them lemonades at a beach stand and they sat on an isolated bench to drink them and stare out at the water.

After a while, he wrapped his arm around her, and she leaned against him.

And it felt perfect. So good that he didn't want to move, didn't want to leave, didn't want to go back into the real world that would inevitably hurt him.

He knew that feeling was wrong, but he couldn't seem to help it.

"Have you always been this beautiful?" he murmured after a few minutes.

She tilted her head up with a wry smile. "That sounds awfully sappy."

"It wasn't supposed to be sappy. It was supposed to be a real question."

She appeared to think about this. "I don't think I look any different than I used to."

"Then how could I manage to keep my hands off you all these years?"

With a soft chuckle, she pressed her cheek against his chest. "I guess you've always been a man of iron control."

He had been. He knew it was true. He'd been better at controlling himself than anyone. He'd always prided himself on it.

She'd evidently continued thinking about his previous question because she added, "I'm not wearing my hair in a ponytail, and I'm wearing more flattering clothes, but that shouldn't make a huge difference in how I look. I don't think."

She sounded worried about something.

He didn't like the sound of it, so he pressed a kiss into her hair. "You were always beautiful. I just couldn't let myself see it."

This was evidently the right thing to say. He felt her relax.

He stroked her hair as they sat together, and then that didn't feel like enough. So he nuzzled her neck, her jaw, until she turned her head toward him. Then he was able to claim her mouth.

She responded eagerly, with an enthusiasm that thrilled him. She wanted him to kiss her this way. She wanted even more.

His tongue slipped between her lips as she twined her arms around his neck, and his body started to pulse with building need and pleasure.

She was so sweet and so strong and so much of what he wanted.

What he'd always wanted.

And she was giving herself to him completely. No holding back.

His heart could hardly handle the way she was filling it.

He wasn't able to touch her the way he wanted because of their positions on the bench, so he pulled her over on top of him, onto his lap. This was much better. She was pressing her breasts against his chest, and his hands were sliding down to cup her soft bottom.

His body was throbbing now—he'd hardened against her completely—and the desire felt like the whole of existence.

She was making little whimpers and gasps that proved she was feeling it too.

He wanted her to feel even more. He wanted to give her everything.

"John," she panted, her little fingers digging into his back when his mouth traced a path down her neck. "John!"

Nothing in the world had ever sounded better than her saying his name in that helpless way.

He cupped her bottom possessively and pressed her into him more tightly. The pressure on his groin made him groan.

"John." She was saying his name again. Something had changed about it, but his mind was so filled with her, with this visceral need, that he couldn't think through what was different.

She'd moved her hands to his shoulders as he rocked his hips into hers.

"John," she said again. This time the word was paired with a little push.

The push broke through his heated stupor, and he dropped his hands from her body with a gasp. He stared at her flushed, rumpled face above his and tried to figure out what was happening.

The only thing he was aware of was his body was roaring with need and frustration, and there was no way to satisfy it now that she'd stopped them.

"We need to slow down a little," she rasped, breathing so heavily he could see her chest rising and falling. "We need to... slow down."

Of course they did.

Of course they did.

What the hell had he been thinking, making out with her in that way on a public bench on a beach?

"Yeah," he managed to pant, his groin aching painfully at the loss of pressure, friction, relief. "Yeah. Sorry."

She awkwardly climbed off his lap and sat down on the bench beside him again. "It's... not a big deal."

It felt like a big deal. It felt terrible.

And then it felt even worse as he realized that she'd been trying to stop him for a while before he'd managed to let go of her.

"Sorry," he said again. "Shit. I'm sorry, Bets."

"You don't have to be sorry. We just got carried away. It's fine."

"How long... how long were trying to get me off you before I listened?"

She rolled her eyes at him. "I wasn't trying to get you off me. I was trying to slow us down a little. Don't be ridiculous."

He didn't think he was being ridiculous. He knew exactly how he'd been feeling.

He'd lost control. Completely.

He never did that.

He didn't want to be the kind of man who did that.

Bad things happened when men lost control of themselves.

Very bad things.

"I'm sorry," he said again. There wasn't anything else he could say.

"Stop saying that."

"Okay."

They sat for a few minutes in silence except for their labored breathing. Eventually John's body stopped screaming at him, although he was still uncomfortably aware of being brutally unsatisfied.

"Are you okay?" she asked at a last, her voice soft and anxious.

"Yes. I'm fine. A man who acts like he can't hold himself back because of his physical condition is a liar and a jackass."

She chuckled at this, evidently feeling better. "I didn't mean about that. I mean about... everything."

"I'm fine," he said again, although he didn't mean it quite as much this time.

"All right. If you're okay to walk, I guess we should be getting back. I feel like I might be getting too much sun."

"Sure." He stood up. His body was pretty much back under control, but nothing else felt normal or controlled about him.

Something was wrong.

Terribly wrong.

Heartbreakingly wrong.

He just hadn't wrapped his mind around what it was yet.

They walked in silence, and Betsy reached for his hand. He let her hold it, but even that felt too torturously close to her.

If he wasn't careful, he would drag her against him again, draw her down onto the sand, kiss her breathless, find carnal satisfaction in her body.

He was so close to doing so it was terrifying.

"You okay?" she asked as they were nearing Balm in Gilead.

"Yes. Are you?"

"I'm fine."

"Good."

Inane, clichéd conversation that conveyed almost nothing real. Because what was real couldn't really be said.

John's mind was in an uproar as they made their way back up the walkway toward the building.

"Oh, I have something in the car for you," Betsy said. "I'll run get it before we sit down."

She was planning to stay here all afternoon, the way she had the past couple of days.

And John desperately wanted her to and desperately needed her to leave at exactly the same time.

He sat down in one of the stiff chairs in the lobby while he waited. He could have gone with her to her car, but he felt like he needed a couple of minutes to pull himself together.

He was staring blindly at a spot in the lobby when a familiar figure crossed his line of vision.

Vivian, that woman he'd met the other day.

She was dressed in the same expensive, professional way as when he'd last seen her and carrying that same leather bag.

She'd been leaving Cecily's office, but she paused when she saw him and waved. "Hi again," she said with a smile.

He smiled automatically, in the way people did when someone greeted them. "Hello. Back again, are you?"

She walked over. "I was just making the arrangements for our retreat this fall. Jeff talked me into it."

He nodded. "It will be a good place for it."

"How long are you staying here?"

"Just a couple more days."

"And you still haven't used a phone or computer?"

"Nope."

"That must take some major willpower."

150

He gave a little shrug. He wasn't sure anyone should be complimenting him on his willpower at the moment.

"You sure you don't want to borrow my phone?" she asked, her light tone almost playful as she offered him her expensive smartphone.

She was teasing, he knew, but he stared at the phone for a long time. In a strange way, it was a manifestation of the real world, the one he knew was waiting for him when he left this place.

The lurking wave waiting to crash into him, drown him.

Maybe things would fall into place better once he reacquainted himself with the world.

"You're really thinking about it," Vivian said, her expression changing. She unlocked the screen of her phone and tapped an icon to pull up an app. "You can pull something up on the web browser, if you really want to. I don't believe in separation from one's phone."

He shouldn't.

He knew he shouldn't.

But he shouldn't do a lot of things he'd been doing this week.

He took the phone and pulled up a search on the web version of his email. "Thanks," he murmured. "I'll just check my email real quick. It's been almost two weeks."

"I hate to think what would pile up in my in-box if I didn't check in for two weeks."

John was too absorbed in the subject lines of emails to respond.

They'd all been read. Betsy had been checking his email, exactly as he'd asked her to.

She must have been clearing out the junk, newsletters, and irrelevant stuff since there were fewer than twenty emails remaining.

Messages from a few of his friends. Some updates and informational items from work that he could look at later.

When he saw an email near the bottom of the list from one of their other team members, with the subject line "Jamal," he clicked on it.

He blinked several times at the three lines of text in the message, sent to their entire team.

Jamal died last night. We aren't telling John until he's left the retreat center. It's going to hit him hard.

John's eyes clouded over as he processed the words.

He wondered if he was supposed to have received that email at all. Or maybe Betsy was supposed to have deleted it.

It didn't matter now.

"Everything all right?" Vivian asked, her voice breaking through the fog in his brain.

He gave a little jerk, logged out of his email, and then closed the browser app. "Yeah. Yeah. Sorry. Thanks for letting me check."

Her forehead wrinkled slightly as she peered at him, as if she suspected something was wrong, but they were basically strangers, so she didn't pursue the matter. "No problem. I'm happy to help out another soul lost without his phone."

She smiled and gave him a little wave as she left the lobby.

John sat down again, his body pulsing as intensely as it had been doing earlier on the bench with Betsy but for a very different reason.

Jamal was dead.

He'd been a sweet, smart boy who loved American culture. He'd loved to laugh.

He'd never laugh anymore.

That was the real world. The true world. The one he'd always known had been lurking, waiting for him, ready to attack him as soon as he left the doors of his place.

The real world where people were hurting while he was lost in his indulgent idyll here for the past two weeks.

He was suddenly aware that Betsy was standing in front of him.

Betsy was part of that idyll too.

"John?" she asked.

He blinked up at her, noticing she was carrying what looked like a small canvas. "What do you have?" An irrelevant question but the only thing he could think of to say.

She gave him a sheepish smile as she handed it to him. "I saw this at a shop this morning and thought of you."

He stared down at the oil painting—a very fine one of a man on a gray horse on the beach, too far in the distance to see his face. The scenery of sea and sky behind him were beautiful and tumultuous, and the man's figure stood out starkly against them.

A man on a horse.

Like the knight from the daydreams she used to have.

His stomach almost heaved. "This isn't me," he muttered.

"I know." She sounded confused. "I just saw it and thought of you. You don't have to keep it if you don't like it, if you think it's silly."

He did like it. It embodied everything he desperately wanted, everything he knew he couldn't have.

"It's not me."

She seemed to droop in front of him as she laid the canvas on the chair he'd just stood up from. "Then just forget it. What's wrong, John?"

"What do you mean?"

"I mean it looks like someone has hit you with a sledgehammer. What's wrong?"

He suddenly remembered Jamal again.

"Someone lent me her phone."

"What?" Betsy's voice was slightly sharp. "No one should have a phone here. You're not supposed to be on it."

"I know. But I checked my email."

He was watching, so he saw the bleak recognition as it passed over her face.

"I know about Jamal," he said.

She took a deep breath. "I'm so sorry, John." She reached out for him, but he pulled his arm away so she couldn't touch him.

"You didn't tell me." The words came out as a gruff accusation. He didn't want to sound so mean, but something was happening here, and he couldn't shy away from it.

Not anymore.

Not just because he wanted to so much.

"I know." She took a shaky breath. "I'm sorry about that. But I did call Chuck, and he said it was better not to tell you until you leave here. We didn't... We were trying to make sure you got some rest."

"I'm not a child who needs to be protected from the world."

"I never said you were a child. John, would you please look me in the eye? Let's go somewhere more private so we can talk about this."

He shook his head, very clear about what he needed to do now. Painfully clear. "No."

"No, you don't want to talk?"

"No, we don't need to go anywhere else. I think it's probably better if you leave." He made his tone as gentle as possible since he didn't want the words to sound like a blow.

Betsy obviously took them as one anyway. Her features twisted in pain. "John, please. I understand you're angry, but—"

"I'm not angry. I understand why you did what you did."

"But we need to talk about it. If this relationship is ever going to work, then we need to figure out how to—"

"It's not." Those words too were gentle, almost soft.

She sucked in a sharp breath and went pale. "What?"

"It's not going to work. Not long-term. It's just something that happened this week."

"John, you don't mean that. I get that you're upset about Jamal, but—"

"It's not about Jamal. I've been thinking about it. It's not going to last past this week. I shouldn't have let it happen to begin with."

She was dead white now, and she couldn't keep her mouth steady. "I don't understand," she said hoarsely. "Things were going well. Is it about what happened earlier? On the bench? Because I told you—"

"It's not about any of that." He needed to end this conversation soon or he was going to completely lose it, take everything back and tell her he was desperately in love with her.

He would stop being the good man he'd always tried to be.

"John—"

"I'm sorry, Bets. You took this more seriously than I did, and I don't want to string you along. I should have put a stop to it earlier."

He knew how cruel those words were to say. He could see it on her face. She swayed on her feet briefly before she looked away from him with a jerk of her head.

Her features were working, trying to control her emotion.

She was very close to crying.

Because of him.

He'd been wrong about himself from the beginning. He was evidently the kind of man he hated.

The kind of man to indulge himself at the expense of a woman. The kind of man to leave her heartbroken when he came to his senses.

"Okay," she said at last. Her voice broke on the last syllable, and she took a ragged breath.

Then she squared her shoulders. "Okay."

And that was all she said. She turned around and walked away.

He watched her leave, her lush curves still prompting a visceral response in his body. Despite everything, he couldn't stop wanting her.

But it was better this way.

The two weeks were almost over, and he could go back to feeling decent about himself, sure that he was doing good in the world. Not basking in sunshine and forgetting about what selfishness could lead to.

He'd learned that lesson all too well at sixteen.

And now he was learning it again.

Maybe eventually he'd get to the point where he wasn't constantly learning it.

He glanced behind him and saw that Betsy had left the little oil painting. He stared down at the man on the horse, silhouetted against a stormy sky.

She thought that was him, but she was wrong.

It could never be him.

ELEVEN

When Betsy got back home, her mother was out of the house. She'd left a note on the kitchen counter.

> *Gone to eat at Linda's. Stew in fridge to warm up for you. Love, Mom.*

Betsy stood staring down at the scrawled note and had to fight against tears.

She managed to control herself, and she kept busy for the next hour. She wiped down the counters and mopped the floors and took the garbage out.

If only she could fill her mind with other things, the ball of grief inside her wouldn't unleash.

Her mother kept a fairly clean house, so soon there weren't any other chores left to do. It was almost seven in the evening, and the world felt bleak and lonely and empty.

And John had broken up with her, leaving absolutely no hope for a future together.

She was sitting on the couch in the living room doing nothing when her mother came home.

Her mother put her purse and keys on the entryway table. "Honey, before I forget, Linda asked if you wanted to help out with the bridal shower she's throwing for Marcy."

A bridal shower.

That was something that happened to other women, along with marriage and children and family and life lived with someone else.

It wasn't something that ever happened to her.

Betsy couldn't move, couldn't speak.

Her mother paused as she stepped into the living room. "Betsy?"

Betsy just stared, frozen like a piece of ice, that ball of grief trembling, pulsing inside her.

"Honey, what happened? What's wrong?"

Even after she opened her mouth, no words came out to explain.

Her mother's face changed. "Did something happen with John?"

"Please don't tell me I told you so," Betsy managed to rasp as the ball of grief finally exploded. Her shoulders shook with silent sobs.

She'd tried to be smart. She'd tried to be careful. She'd tried to protect her heart.

But she'd trusted John. She hadn't thought she needed to protect her heart from *him*.

"Oh, honey." Her mother came over and sat down next to her on the couch, pulling her into a hug. "I'm so, so sorry. I know exactly how it feels."

~

Betsy spent the next day crying and praying and cocooned in the house. That was only to be expected, so she wasn't too frustrated or disappointed in herself. She'd had a real emotional blow, and she would need some time to recover.

But the next day she expected to feel a little better. Just a little—but enough to give her some hope.

She didn't feel any better though. If anything, she felt worse. She had to start going through the rest of her life. She couldn't stay holed up in her mother's house, cut off from the rest of the world.

And she was going to have to start doing it without John.

It would be easier for her if she could just be angry with him, but the truth was she understood exactly what had happened.

He'd been trying something different. He'd been trying to let go of the rigid control he'd always kept on himself and the world. And then he'd gotten scared when he'd realized how much faith it took to live that way.

He wasn't a cruel man who had taken advantage of her feelings. He wasn't a selfish man who did what he felt like doing with a woman and then dropped her as soon as he got bored.

John was a good man. But he was flawed like everyone else. And he didn't know how to change.

She'd hoped for a few days that he would, that they could change together, but that was obviously not going to happen.

She could understand. She would keep praying for him.

She hoped he was all right.

But what she wasn't going to hope for was for him to change his mind. After the way he'd looked when she'd seen him last, she knew that wasn't going to happen.

With this in mind, she steeled herself to get going with the rest of her life.

The first thing she had to do was call Chuck.

There was a sick feeling in her gut as she found his number on her phone and pressed send. This was it. After this conversation, her whole life would change.

It was going to change, whether she wanted it to or not.

"Hey, Betsy," Chuck said, picking up the call. "How's everything going there?"

"Fine."

Chuck hesitated. "Uh-oh. That doesn't sound good."

"I just said fine."

"I'm good at picking up undertones."

She swallowed, his familiar intelligence and good humor making her throat ache with emotion. "Well, the truth is, I've... I've done some thinking and made some decisions."

"Shit," he breathed. "You're about to resign, aren't you?"

"I'm really sorry. But I think I have to."

"Has something better come along? I hope."

"Not really. I just... I can't do this job anymore. I hate to bail on you like this, but—"

"No, no. Don't apologize. Most people don't do the job you were doing for long. It's really hard on our... our soul. I completely understand."

"Thank you. I mean it. I wish there were some way I could still work for you, but I just can't stay part of the team, so I guess I need to resign."

"Wait, you think you might want to still work for us? Because if so, I'm sure we could find you something at the headquarters in Charlotte. We'd hate to lose you."

Betsy blinked, a little flutter of pleasure in her chest, despite the cloud of grief that still surrounded her. "Really? There might be some way for me to work from there?"

"Sure! If you were interested, we could figure out something. We were going to add a couple of administrative positions there in the next year anyway, so we could probably craft a position that would work for you—focused on communication. You'd have to do some supervision and management though—mostly volunteers and interns. I don't know if you'd be interested in that."

"I wouldn't mind that at all. That sounds wonderful. I didn't even dream something like that would work out."

"Of course. We want to take care of our people, and that often means moving them around. There might be some traveling with the new position, but it wouldn't be more than a few times a year."

"That would be great. Perfect. Thank you so much."

"Sure. I'll talk to Curtis about it, and we'll work it out." He paused for a moment. "Have you told John?"

She had to take a breath before she answered, "I'm going to talk to him today."

"Okay. Okay. I'll wait until tomorrow before I call him to talk about it."

"Thanks."

"How's he doing?"

"I... I don't know."

"Shit," he breathed again. "Okay. I guess these things happen."

Betsy didn't know how he'd figured out what happened between her and John from nothing more than this cryptic conversation, but he obviously had a pretty good idea.

"I'll be in touch soon about the new position," he added.

"Okay. Thanks again."

She hung up, sad and sick and feeling just a little better that she'd started making some needed decisions, necessary changes.

A job in the headquarters in Charlotte would be perfect. She could still contribute in valuable ways to a cause she believed in, but she wouldn't have to be a member of John's team anymore.

She had to talk to him today. She couldn't delay it any longer.

He would be leaving Balm in Gilead this afternoon to spend two weeks with his brother. And Chuck was going to call him.

If she didn't tell him her decision today, Chuck would tell him tomorrow.

~

An hour later, she was getting out of her car in the parking lot when a voice caught her attention.

It was saying her name.

She looked around and saw Mark hurrying down the front walk from the building.

She stopped and waved at him. He'd obviously come to pick up John as they'd planned from the beginning.

When Mark was close enough for them to speak, he said, "Thank God you're here. What's going on?"

"What do you mean?"

"John looks like he's a walking corpse, but he won't tell me anything. Please tell me what's going on." Mark's face was anxious, and it hurt Betsy's chest.

She kept control of her emotion, however, as she replied, "Oh. I don't know. I haven't talked to him for two days."

"What? I thought you two were—" Mark broke off his words, his face twisting with recognition. "Shit," he said, almost exactly like Chuck had earlier. "Shit, you two broke up?"

"We were never really together."

He gave her an impatient look.

"Really," she said. "I mean, he'd never made a conscious decision about it, and now he has."

"So this is his fault?"

She cleared her throat. "It's nobody's fault. He has his reasons."

"I can just imagine how stupid his reasons are." He shook his head with a long sigh. Then turned his eyes back to her face again. "How are you? Are you doing okay?"

The question was such a small gesture of real kindness that Betsy's eyes burned with tears. That instinctive kindness clearly ran in the family. "I'm okay. I'm not going to say I'm not sad about it, but he's just not ready for it. I don't know if he'll ever really be. And I just can't wait around."

"Of course you can't. He's an idiot." Despite the words, Mark obviously wasn't annoyed by his brother. His face reflected real worry. "I know how he feels about you."

She gave a little shrug. "That's not always enough. If you don't mind, I need to talk to him in private for a minute. Can I go on up?"

"Sure. I was just bringing the car around to the front to load his stuff up. I'll wait for... a half hour?"

"Not that long. Just give me fifteen minutes."

Fifteen minutes. That was as long as it would take. Then it would be done.

She had to do this. She *had* to. Even if it tore her apart.

She stiffened her spine and resolved her will and made her way into the building and then up to the top floor.

The door to John's room was halfway open, so she tapped on it and took a step in.

The room was picked up, his luggage all packed. He was just coming out of the bathroom. "If you'll just grab the package on the bed, I can get the rest of my st—" He broke off with a visible start when he saw it was her and not Mark, whom he'd obviously been expecting.

He looked pale beneath his tan, and there were deep shadows under his eyes. He'd looked so happy and rested earlier this week, and now he looked worse than he'd been when they'd first arrived here.

She gave him a little smile. "Hi."

"Hi." He didn't smile at all. He just gazed at her soberly.

"I just stopped by for a minute," she said.

A faint relief reflected on his face, and she realized he'd been afraid she'd come to beg for him to take her back.

Despite everything, that hurt, the knowledge that he thought she had that little sense, that little pride.

She brushed the stray thought away and continued, "I just needed to talk to you, and I wanted to do it face-to-face."

His brow lowered. "About what?"

"About the team." Surely he would know they needed to have a discussion about her job. Surely he didn't think she'd keep working for him, after everything that had happened. "About my job."

"What about it?"

"I talked to Chuck this morning. He's going to try to get me some sort of position in Charlotte."

"What? *What?* Why?"

Her eyes widened. "I can't keep working with you, John. You must know that."

He opened his mouth, but the flare of emotion she'd caught in his eyes pulled itself back into tight control. He gave a stiff little nod. "Okay."

"Okay? I know this is awkward and... and hard, but it's the only decision I can make. I've been rethinking things anyway, and I think it's the right decision for me now in every way. I'll miss... I'll miss the team. And I've appreciated working with you more than you can know."

"Same here." The words were almost gruff, but she knew that he meant them.

This was as good as they were going to do with a farewell. She needed to get out of here while she could.

When she was alone, she could cry a little and then hopefully start to recover.

"Okay. Anyway, I just wanted to tell you in person. Chuck said he'd call you tomorrow."

"Good. If that's what you want, then I'm glad it will work out."

She could tell he was forcing the words out, and she couldn't stand much more of this. She wanted to hug him. She wanted to comfort him. She wanted to help him let go, let down his guard.

But he wasn't going to let her do that. Not again.

She sighed and turned toward the door. "Goodbye, John. Take care of yourself."

"You too."

She took a step toward the door and then another. Then she paused when she noticed a wrapped package on the bed.

It was exactly the size of the oil painting she'd given him.

He'd kept it. He'd wrapped it in brown paper to protect it. He was taking it with him.

The world blurred around her for a moment as her knees went weak. Then she blew out a breath and continued her walk to the door.

She'd stepped over the threshold when she turned her head to look at him one more time. He was standing with slumped shoulders and downcast eyes. He looked so incredibly lonely that her heart went out with him.

She said, "I hope you'll remember how it felt on the boat the other day. That's what joy is really about."

He lifted his eyes but didn't speak, didn't move.

She closed the door behind her as she left.

~

In the lobby, she noticed Cecily and Zeke standing just outside the door to the office. Something was strange in the air between them as they turned toward her presence, and she wondered if they'd been arguing.

Cecily wasn't the type who really argued. She just blissfully went through life, doing as she thought best and expecting the rest of the world to fall in line. And Zeke didn't seem to talk enough to argue for real.

But they worked together. She imagined they must have occasional disagreements.

The thought was a pleasant distraction from the flood of tears that was coiled inside her, and she waved as Cecily smiled at her.

Betsy would have preferred to get out of the building quickly, but she stopped when Cecily walked over to her.

"How are you doing?" Cecily asked, her voice low so Zeke couldn't hear it across the room.

"I'm fine." Betsy forced a smile.

"John was doing so well until a couple of days ago. I'm really sorry things didn't work out between you two."

Damn it. It felt absolutely terrible—for everyone in the world to know about her broken heart. "Thanks."

"Relationships don't always work out when they're started here. For a number of reasons. But I really thought you two would. You two were perfectly matched."

Betsy cleared her throat. "Thanks."

It surprised her—a lot—that she actually agreed with Cecily's assessment. She and John were good together. Really good. They brought out the best in each other.

She no longer thought that John was an amazing catch and wouldn't give her a passing glance. He didn't dump her because she wasn't good enough for him.

He thought he wasn't good enough for her.

It was a strange and revealing recognition, and it washed over Betsy with its power.

She had changed.

She really had.

And she wasn't going to change back.

"Sorry," Cecily said with a wry smile. "I'm sure this is the last thing you want to hear. You probably just want to get out of here. I just wanted to say something. I hope you'll keep in touch, whenever you're visiting your mom."

"I will. Thank you."

When she walked out of the building, she saw Mark in his car on the front drive. She waved to him and managed to smile.

He waved back and got out to go in and help his brother bring his stuff down.

This was an ending.

You didn't always know when that was happening in life, but sometimes you did. Sometimes you knew when things were drawing to a close, when everything would change from that moment on.

And this was one of those times.

~

A week later, Betsy was propped up on the pillows on the bed in her mother's guest room with her laptop on her thighs.

She'd done errands with her mother that morning and then had lunch with Dennis.

She'd made it clear she wasn't ready for romance at the moment—or anytime soon, as far as her heart was concerned—but she genuinely liked the man and wanted to at least be friendly with him.

He seemed to understand and hadn't been pushy or obnoxious about it.

It was nice to know there were men like that in the world. A lot of them. Good, kindhearted men who wanted the best for her.

John was one of them, although he wouldn't let himself be any more than that to her.

He was in Willow Park now, visiting with his brother.

She really hoped he was all right. She hoped he wouldn't forget what he'd learned over the past two weeks about enjoying life, enjoying God, letting himself be more than just a series of duties.

She prayed for him briefly before she went back to searching for possible apartments to rent in Charlotte.

Chuck had been as good as his word, and they'd crafted a position with her in mind, one that would take in a lot of responsibilities that they'd needed someone to cover anyway.

Things were working out the way they were supposed to. It might not be what Betsy had really wanted, but life didn't often offer that. What it did offer was good. She loved her work, and she was going to love her new job.

She was even a little bit excited about having a new start.

If she didn't miss John so much, she might even be happy about it.

She lowered her laptop with a frown when she heard her mother's voice was outside.

"Betsy! Betsy! Get out here! Quick!"

Something must be wrong. Her mother never shouted like that.

Betsy scrambled off the bed, leaving her laptop open on the covers, and ran down the hall, into the living room, and then out to the front lawn, where her mother's voice had come from.

Her mom looked okay. She was standing on the front step, staring at something on the street.

Once she'd assured herself of her mother's health and safety, Betsy turned to look too.

She froze.

For a moment she was sure that she was dreaming, imagining. Because things like this simply didn't happen in real life.

But the sun was hot on her skin, and her mother was breathing heavily beside her.

Betsy's bare feet burned on the pavement.

And John Davenport was on the street in front of the house, sitting astride a gray horse.

He was holding on to the reins, and his expression was like nothing she'd ever seen before. Almost naked with a mingling of emotions—tenderness, self-consciousness, anxiety, hesitation, regret, amusement.

Betsy's mouth dropped open. "What... What..."

"Don't be silly, honey," her mother said, giving Betsy a gentle shove toward the street. "He's obviously here for you. He's finally made his decision."

There could be no other explanation. Absolutely no other way to make sense of this.

John's horse stepped a few times nervously.

Betsy stumbled toward him.

Then John looked down at her. "You can go ahead and laugh if you want to," he said.

Betsy didn't laugh.

She burst into tears, right there in her mother's front yard.

TWELVE

John had been having a very bad week.

First he'd had to make it through a painful car ride across the state to Willow Park with Mark, who was clearly unhappy with him.

Mark didn't say anything for the first couple of hours of the trip. He'd just kept shooting John frustrated and questioning looks.

John had felt numb, almost frozen, as if the slightest blow would crack him. He couldn't talk. He could barely keep taking even breaths. Betsy's devastated face when he'd told her he'd never been serious about them kept materializing behind his eyelids, every time he closed his eyes.

He wasn't even going to be able to see her at work anymore.

He wasn't going to ever see her again.

It wasn't a truth he was able to fully process and still hold on to his control, so he kept pushing it from his mind as he stared out the window of the car at the changing scenery. Beach to hills to mountains. Plus a thousand other cars on the interstate, all of them living their lives, going about their business, unaware that John's heart had been utterly shattered.

Finally Mark burst out without warning, "Damn it, John!"

John jerked in surprise. "What was that for?"

He knew what it was for. He just didn't want to have the conversation.

"You're an idiot."

"You don't know what's going on."

"Betsy told me. I know exactly what's going on. You fell in love with her, and now you're scared of actually being happy for the first time since Mom and Dad died."

John felt his face grow pale and a chill tighten in his chest. "She told you that?"

"No. She told me you dumped her. I just extrapolated the rest because I'm clever that way." His tone was sharply ironic.

"I didn't dump her. We were never really going out."

"That's a flimsy excuse, and you know it perfectly well. You had something good, and then you threw it away because—I don't know—because you're still eaten up with guilt for no good reason."

"It's not that. Not really."

"Then what is it?"

"I don't really have time or emotional energy for a relationship. My job is too important."

Mark rolled his eyes. "Do you have any idea how ridiculous that sounds?"

"I don't care if it sounds ridiculous." John's tone had an edge to it, but he needed this conversation to end very soon or he would totally lose it. "It's the truth."

"It wasn't your fault that Mom and Dad died."

"I know that," John growled. "I'm not a fool."

"Yes, you are. Because you know it in your head, but you're still acting on it like it's true. You can do your duty, you can serve God, you can be the person you want to be, and still be happy with Betsy."

John wished that were true. He'd believed it was true for a few days.

But it wasn't.

There was no argument he could give Mark though, so he sat in stony silence.

"You're an idiot," Mark muttered.

That could very well be true. But John still knew he was right.

~

It would be easier to be right if it didn't make him so miserable.

For the next three days, he spent his time visiting with Mark and Sophie, hanging out with their friends, doing some work around the charming old Craftsman house in a pleasant Willow Park neighborhood they'd just bought, and he pretended that everything was all right.

He knew Mark wasn't convinced, and he suspected Sophie was worried about him because she kept trying to coddle him with good food and creature comforts. But he assured himself that no one else he encountered knew that every moment without Betsy felt like a loss.

On Thursday morning, he took a long walk alone, spending most of the time praying and trying to get his mind and feelings back under control. He was on his way back to the house when he paused on seeing a little fair-haired boy on a tricycle riding furiously in his direction. John wasn't any good at guessing children's ages, but he supposed this boy was maybe three.

If the boy didn't stop, he would run right into John.

"Nathaniel!" a voice called out from farther down the block. "Slow down and watch where you're going. The whole sidewalk doesn't belong to you."

The boy stopped pedaling and turned to look back to his father.

His father was Daniel Duncan.

John smiled and waved to the other man as he approached.

"Sorry about that," Daniel said, turning the boy around so he was riding in the opposite direction.

"No problem. He's doing pretty good for his age."

"Yeah. He's begging to ride a real bike, but he's a little too young yet, I think." Daniel seemed to assure himself that his son was still in sight and then walked over to John. "How's your week been going?"

"Good. Fine. Good." Okay, that didn't sound very convincing.

Daniel didn't comment on the dubious answer. "How long are you staying?"

"For two weeks."

"And then back to the field after that?"

"Yes."

Daniel's expression was casual, but John suspected the other man knew more than he let on. Maybe Mark had talked to him, or maybe he was just good at reading people.

This suspicion was confirmed when Daniel continued, "How's Betsy?"

"She's fi—" John broke off his automatic reply because he wasn't at all sure it was true. He didn't know if Betsy was fine. He didn't know if she was hurting as much as he was. He didn't know if she hated him now, if she never wanted to see him again.

He didn't know anything.

Daniel cocked an eyebrow at him.

John shrugged. "I don't know how she is. I haven't talked to her lately."

"Oh. That's too bad. I like her a lot."

"Yeah." He had too. John had more than liked her.

He'd loved her, and he'd broken her heart just the same.

"Do you ever think about getting out of the field?" Daniel asked, still casual as if this were just normal conversation and not twisting John's heart into a vice.

He blinked. "No. Why would I?"

"I don't know. It's pretty normal, I'd think. After so many years, that kind of work starts to beat people down."

"I guess. But not me. This is… this is who I am. This is what I've been called to do."

Daniel nodded. "I know how that feels."

"Do you?"

"Of course. Why wouldn't I?"

"Has anyone ever suggested you get out of the ministry because it's hard on you?"

Daniel gave him a little smile, evidently unaffected by the blunt question. "Yes. A lot of people. The church I was in before this one folded. It completely fell apart. It was hard not to blame myself, and a lot of people told me I should just do something else—at least temporarily."

"But you didn't."

"No. I didn't. But it put me in a really bad situation—spiritually and emotionally. My first wife had died a couple of years earlier, and with that plus the church falling apart, it felt like God was punishing me, like I deserved to be unhappy. Then I started to fall in love with Jessica, and all those underlying spiritual issues came to the surface. Being happy with her made me feel horribly guilty, and so I kept pushing her away."

John knew why the other man was telling him this story, but he was interested anyway, so he asked, "So what happened?"

"I got myself right with God, and then I got myself right with Jessica. Or rather, she forgave me." He chuckled. Then noticed that Nathaniel had reached the end of the block. "Nathaniel! Back this way!"

They both watched as the little boy turned around and started back toward them.

"Things aren't right all the time now, of course, but I'm really happy. And I can be happy without guilt, so that's definite progress."

John couldn't even remember what it felt like to be happy without guilt.

But he wanted it.

He wanted it desperately.

"Mine's not a spiritual issue," he heard himself murmuring. He was mostly speaking to himself, so he didn't know why he'd said it out loud.

Daniel gave him a quick look although he was still smiling. "We tell ourselves that. It's just a circumstantial issue. Or a vocational issue. Or an emotional one. But they're all spiritual issues at heart. I know you already know this, but sometimes it's good to hear it again. When Jesus came to do his duty—I'm not even sure it was his duty; it was ours, and we just couldn't do it—but when he came to do the will of God, he didn't just do a job. He lived out his love. He died out of love." He paused for a moment before he concluded softly, "His work was love."

The words hit him hard, making his hands shake, but John frowned anyway. "Do you always pretend to tell personal stories when you're really trying to make a point to someone?"

Daniel laughed out loud. "My first instinct is always to give a theological lecture, so just be glad I've gotten past that."

John chuckled too—it was really hard to stay annoyed with the man—and then waved goodbye to Daniel and his son.

He kept walking back to Mark and Sophie's house, and his mind was filled with questions.

Betsy had told him he had spiritual issues to work out.

Mark had told him the same thing.

He'd actually come to the same conclusion himself on the boat with Betsy last week. He'd felt what it was like to take joy in life, in God, in creation, without an overpowering sense of guilt and responsibility.

But then he'd fallen right back into his old way of thinking.

Maybe there was some way to get back there.

He really wanted to.

~

He kept thinking and praying about it for the next three days until he couldn't think of anything else.

On Sunday, he was sitting at the kitchen table with Mark, drinking coffee. Sophie was in her room getting dressed, so the two men were sitting alone, in silence.

Mark said without warning, "So have you finally figured it out yet?"

John looked up at his brother, blinking in surprise. "Figured out what?"

"Look, I've tried to be patient because I know how long it sometimes takes to work through things. I took way longer myself. But I'm really getting annoyed. You know you're wrong. You *know* it. You just don't want to admit it."

A week ago, John would have been so angered by this pronouncement that he would have just gotten up and left the table. But today it simply crystalized what he'd been chewing on for the past few days. "I think it's too late," he said at last.

Mark's eyebrows lifted as if he hadn't expected this response. "No, it's not. It's not too late."

"I treated her... terribly."

"She loves you. She'll forgive you."

"What if she doesn't?" He couldn't believe he was asking that. He couldn't believe he was talking as if he'd already made his decision.

But maybe he had.

Mark was right. John knew he was wrong. He knew he'd been letting fear and guilt blind him into pushing away the best thing that had come into his life in years.

He knew he'd been trying to earn God's favor so he wouldn't make him suffer again the way he'd suffered when his parents had died. He knew how wrong that was. How utterly irrational.

He wanted to live out his faith for real.

He wanted to love.

He wanted to love Betsy.

"Then at least you tried. Do you really want to live the rest of your life having just let her go?"

John shook his head, staring down at his coffee. "No. I really don't."

"So go get her. Do whatever you need to do to prove to her that she's more important than your guilt and your fear and your hang-ups. That she's more important than who you were before."

John looked up, staring at his brother blindly as an idea came into his mind. A crazy idea. A ridiculous one.

But Betsy didn't believe her old romantic daydreams could ever come true. She didn't believe she was that kind of person.

She'd never thought she was the kind of woman that men would love so much.

And he wanted to prove she was wrong about that—and right about everything else.

"You have an idea," Mark breathed, starting to look excited.

"Yes."

"Then do it. Do it right now. Because, I swear, if you don't stop stewing about this soon, I'm going to kick you out of this house."

~

So that was how John ended up in front of Betsy's mother's house, riding a gray horse on a street in a quiet neighborhood like an absolute idiot.

The horse was a fairly gentle one since it had been years since John had ridden, but it was nervous on the street, even in the neighborhood where no one was driving by. It stepped restlessly while John did his best to speak nice and calm it down until Betsy appeared.

When she came down the sidewalk and burst into tears, the horse obviously decided it was a crisis. She jumped into a trot, and John almost fell off in his attempt to get the horse to stop.

He was aware that Betsy's tears had turned into laughter by the time he'd barely kept his seat and then finally slid off the saddle.

Betsy threw herself into his arms, and he concluded that all the hassle and embarrassment was worth it.

He hugged her back, as tightly as he could, and it was a few minutes before she stopped laughing or crying or the combination of both.

She pulled away, beaming up at him. "What on earth are you doing with that horse?"

He was trying to maintain some degree of composure, but it was a hopeless effort. He was smiling as much as she was, and it felt like his heart might just beat out of his chest. "You wanted a knight on a horse. I'm a pretty lousy knight, but at least I could try to manage the horse."

Still sniffing, she went over to rub her hand on the horse's muzzle. Naturally, the horse grew still and let out a happy little huff.

Everyone loved Betsy. Even those of the equine variety.

"She's lovely," Betsy murmured.

"She's the best steed I could come up with on short notice."

She turned back to meet his eyes. "You didn't have to do this, you know. You could have just showed up. I would have been just as happy. I mean, if this means…"

When she faltered, he knew he'd been so distracted he hadn't even told her the most important thing.

He'd planned the whole thing out for twenty-four hours, but now that he was put on the spot, he felt awkward and tongue-tied. "Of course it does," he muttered rather gruffly.

She peered at him through tear-filled eyes, as if to verify he meant what she thought he meant.

He cleared his throat. "I love you. You know that, right? I love you so much it makes me crazy, as you've probably concluded from my pathetic behavior."

She took a deep breath and let it out, something washing over her face. Relief. Joy. The slightest bit of amusement.

"Damn it," he grumbled. "I'm obviously terrible at this. But I was wrong—incredibly wrong about everything. I was scared and guilty and caught up in my own spiritual... spiritual wrongness that I couldn't even see what was right. But loving you can't be wrong. It can't be a distraction from my calling. It has to be one of the things I was put on earth to do because it's what I want to do more than anything else."

Her mouth dropped open slightly at this earnest declaration, so he figured he must have started to pull it together a bit.

He went on. "And I totally understand if you're not ready to forgive me—or you are ready to forgive but just not jump into a relationship yet. I messed up. Big time. I let myself... I let myself start to take your heart, and then I just threw it back when I got scared. I'm not going to do that again. If you ever feel like you can trust your heart with me again, I'll never let it go. I promise I won't."

Her features started working as if she were fighting off tears again, so he closed the gap between them and wrapped his arms around her once more. She was warm and soft and shaking and Betsy. She was everything he wanted, everything he'd believed he could never have.

"I love you too, John," she mumbled against his shirt.

At this admission, he tightened his arms so much she whimpered and he had to soften his grip again.

She looked up at him. "I do still trust you. I really did understand what you were going through. I... I would have been okay if you'd decided this wasn't what was right for you. But... but..." She sniffed a couple of times. "I'm really glad it is."

He took her lovely, beaming face in his hands and kissed her. She kissed him back, and he was filled with such joy, such feeling, that it might have gotten out of hand if the horse hadn't stepped restlessly in their direction.

Then he remembered they were on the street, and Betsy's mother was still standing on the stoop of her house.

He turned and waved at her ruefully, his arms still around Betsy.

"Glad you made your decision," her mother called out. "But let's keep things to G-rated in my front yard, please."

Both he and Betsy laughed, and then he was aware of an unpleasant odor.

He grabbed Betsy before she stepped backward into what the horse had dropped on the curb.

"Shit," he said, pulling her away from it.

Betsy giggled as she pressed herself against him.

"I don't know what you were thinking when you were a girl," he told her dryly. "But horses aren't exactly the most romantic thing in the world."

"It was perfect," she whispered. "All of it is perfect." She wrinkled her nose. "But maybe we should get rid of this horse now and go inside."

~

John did get rid of the horse, taking it back to where he'd hired it, and took a hose to clean up the mess beside the curb.

By the time he made it inside the house, Betsy's mother had declared herself to have a very busy schedule so she had gone out for a couple of hours.

John sat on the couch, Betsy cuddled up beside him, and he was suddenly so exhausted he couldn't see straight. He could barely even talk.

It would hardly be appropriate to fall asleep on Betsy, after his big romantic gesture and her forgiveness, so he forced the sleepiness away.

He held her hand with one of his and stroked her hair with the other. Everything felt perfectly right, perfectly at peace, for the first time he could remember.

"I can't believe you didn't make me writhe and suffer a little," he murmured. "I would have deserved it."

"I don't care what you deserve. I would have hesitated if I didn't still trust you. But I've known you for years, John. I know who you are. The truth is, I knew things weren't quite right before, that you still weren't all in, but I ignored those hints and worries because I didn't want them to be true. I know you're all in now. I know I can trust you." She tilted her head to meet his eyes. "I've always believed in you, John. I believe in you now."

He was so overwhelmed that his eyes went blurry. He had to exert more control than he would have expected to lean over and give her a soft, little kiss. "Thank you, sweetheart. I still feel like I don't deserve it, but I guess that's what love is about, isn't it?"

"I think so. I think it is."

He relaxed and closed his eyes.

When he realized he was starting to drift off to sleep again, he blinked and lifted his head from the back of the couch. "So what have you been doing this week?"

"Crying," she told him with a hint of a smile. Before he could act on the flood of regret, she continued, "Don't get stupid about it. By the looks of you, you've suffered more than I have. I actually had a lot to do, getting ready for my new job and moving to Charlotte."

"Oh, yeah. I'm glad that worked out for you." He cleared his throat, almost embarrassed to tell her. "Actually, I've talked to Chuck too."

Her forehead wrinkled. "You have? About my job?"

"No. No! Of course not! I mean, I know I can be bossy and opinionated and all that, but I'd never interfere with your job. I talked to him about my job."

"Your job?" Her lips had parted, and it was clear she'd never dreamed it was possible for him to come to this decision.

"Yeah. Everyone's right about me. You, Mark, everyone. I need a break. I need to do something different— at least temporarily. For my own mental and spiritual health. I need... Well, the truth is I also don't want to be traveling all the time because it means I'd have to be away from you. I want to focus on our relationship right now." He didn't know why, but he was incredibly self-conscious about telling her. He cleared his throat again and stared at the picture on the wall across from them. "So Chuck and I worked it out for me to be transferred to the main office in Charlotte for a while—a year at least. I may want to go back in the field after that, but we can play that by ear when the time comes."

Betsy was so surprised she was almost choking on it. "You're... you're serious?"

"Yes. Yes. I am. It's all worked out. I won't be your boss, of course. We'll both report to Chuck and do totally different jobs. I'm… I'm actually excited about it." He finally turned back to look at her awed face. "It's been a long time since I've been so excited about work. That's obviously a sign that you and Mark were right."

And then Betsy was crying again, hiding her face in his shirt.

It hurt to know that she couldn't believe he would ever prioritize her—or even himself—above his job. And to know she would have been right up until yesterday.

"So we'll both be living in Charlotte?" she asked, rather hoarsely, when the emotion had mostly dissipated.

"Yes."

"I can't wait."

John couldn't wait either.

He closed his eyes and thought about it. Before he knew it, he was dozing off, startled awake when Betsy poked his arm.

Her eyes were brimming with laughter. "I can't believe that here we are in our great romantic reconciliation and you're there falling asleep on me."

He blinked rapidly. "Sorry. Sorry."

She giggled helplessly and cuddled up beside him. "I suppose I should take it as a very good sign—that now you're finally able to rest. You can take a nap if you need to."

"I don't," he told her.

The words weren't exactly true though. He was utterly exhausted from the past few days, the past few weeks, the past few years. And now that he'd finally let go, he couldn't keep his eyes open.

And so he did end up taking a nap on her mother's couch.

EPILOGUE

A week after that, Betsy was carrying two cans of ginger ale and a sleeve of saltine crackers out to the front yard of Mark and Sophie's house in Willow Park.

Sophie was sitting in a lawn chair on the grass, and Betsy walked over to hand the other woman the crackers and one of the ginger ales before she sat down in the second lawn chair.

Sophie was little and dark and pretty, but her face was slightly pale now, and she murmured thanks to Betsy before she tore into the sleeve of saltines.

Betsy sipped her own ginger ale and waited until Sophie had eaten a cracker. When the other woman looked up with a smile, Betsy asked, "You okay?"

"Yes. Fine." Sophie took a few deep breaths. "It's really not terrible, as long as I take preventative measures. Crackers. A lot of crackers."

Betsy cleared her throat. "Am I... am I not supposed to be saying anything about it?"

In the two days she'd been visiting, neither Mark nor Sophie had mentioned Sophie's condition, but it was quite obvious to Betsy that the other woman was pregnant.

Sophie gave Betsy a dimpled little smile. "We're not announcing yet. It's still early. You weren't supposed to know."

Betsy chuckled. "Let me guess. John still has no idea."

Sophie was obviously feeling a little better because she giggled too. She shook her head. "I really think he doesn't know, despite the fact that I throw up almost every morning and Mark treats me like I'm made of crystal."

"Is Mark going to tell him?"

"I'll tell him to. I don't want him to feel bad about not knowing."

After their private laugh at the expense of John's occasional cluelessness, the women turned back to the basketball game going on in the driveway. It was one-on-one with John and Mark, and both men were breathing heavily and sweating hard as John protected the basket from Mark's offense.

"What's the score now?" Betsy asked.

"Still zero to zero."

"Wow! One of them will have to make a basket eventually."

The men had been playing now for over thirty minutes. The brothers were evenly matched—same height, same build, similar level of fitness. Betsy wasn't surprised it was a close game, but she was surprised no one had managed to score yet.

"I think they're both better at defense than offense," Sophie murmured.

"I guess so."

She watched as Mark dribbled up to the net and then winced as John blocked his shot by slamming the ball down to the pavement. She wouldn't have wanted to be on the receiving end of that move.

Both the men were totally into the game and clearly determined to win.

She knew John was having a good time though. She could see it in his face, in his stance, in his eyes.

It made her happy that he was happy.

"Mark is really putting up a fight," Sophie commented, her eyes focused on her husband. "Ever since he... he returned, he hasn't been very competitive—at sports or anything else. I mean, he plays well at anything he tries, but he doesn't seem to want to fight to win."

Betsy's smile sobered slightly. "What happened to him would change anyone."

"I know. I don't care if he's competitive or not. I really don't. I just sometimes notice the difference."

"He seems to be fighting today."

"I know." Sophie smiled again. "Being with John is good for him."

"It's good for John too."

"I'm so glad you two are moving to Charlotte. I'd never want to be selfish or anything, but Mark and I have been praying that you'd make a decision like that. You'll be so close now. We can see you all the time."

The thought made Betsy as happy as it clearly made Sophie. She only knew the other woman slightly, but she already knew they could be friends.

It would be nice to have more people in the world besides her mother whom she could consider family.

She looked back over at the driveway at a burst of sound. Mark had almost scored, but the ball had bounced off the rim.

John was obviously enjoying the near miss, if his teasing taunts at his brother were anything to go by.

"Are you going to miss it, do you think?" Sophie asked.

Betsy had to think for a moment before she caught up to the question. "The job, you mean?"

"Yes. I was just wondering if it would be hard for you to do something else now."

"I don't know. Maybe it will. There was a lot I loved about what I used to do. But it's definitely time for a change. And I think I'm more excited about the transition than saddened by it. I really can't wait to get started at my new job."

"A fresh start is always exciting. That's how Mark and I felt when we bought this house. We'd been living in a little loft apartment above the bookstore for more than a year. I really did love that little place, but it's been even better starting a new life here."

"Yes. It's just like that, I think. I've got a new apartment in Charlotte that I'm excited about it. John's going to just keep his old place. He doesn't really care about his living conditions, and he doesn't see any reason to find something new. But I didn't want to live in a cramped little studio. I got a nice two bedroom near work. Fortunately, it's on the outskirts of the city, so it wasn't too expensive. It's going to take me a while to furnish the whole thing since I have almost no furniture, but I wanted two bedrooms for when my mom comes to visit."

"Is she excited for you?"

"She's so excited she calls me every day to hash out everything." Betsy chuckled. "Pretty soon, it's going to start to get a little annoying."

Sophie was about to answer, but a loud roar from the driveway interrupted her. Betsy turned her head in time to see the ball John had just thrown swoosh through the net.

John was grinning and raising his arms above his head and shouting, "Victory!" at the top of his lungs.

Betsy felt a warm flood of pleasure at the sight of his uninhibited behavior. He was almost never like this. He needed to be a lot more.

Mark grumbled and groused—all in good fun—and they clearly decided that the first score decided the game because both the men limped over, hot, tired, and soaked with perspiration. John's shirt was so wet it was nearly transparent.

"Did you see that?" John demanded, stepping closer to her as she stood up.

"Yes. I saw it. It was a brilliant piece of athletic prowess, and other men can only hope to achieve such heights of glory." When John's eyes warmed and he reached out for her, she held up her hands in warning. "No way! You're covered in sweat, and there will be no touching me until you've taken a shower."

"But you look so pretty in that top."

"Shower first."

Mark clapped John on the back. "We have two bathrooms in this house. We're living in the lap of luxury now. No waiting to take your shower."

Mark folded and carried the chairs back in as they all trooped back into the house.

Betsy shooed John away into the guest bathroom, and she could still hear him mock complaining about the rejection behind the closed door.

The house had four bedrooms and two bathrooms, and the one she was staying in was a cute, tiny space with a single bed, a small dresser, and not much else. She went into it to brush out her hair and check her face, and she was pleased to see she looked pretty and rosy from the sun.

She'd bought some new clothes in the past few days. Not a huge number, and all of them were on sale, but compared to her normal buying habits, it felt like a shopping spree.

But she wanted to branch out from wearing nothing but jeans, T-shirts, and ponytails. She wanted to wear things that were pretty and flattering and not just "basic."

191

She didn't just want to be pretty for John. She wanted to be pretty for herself.

She was content and smiling as she went into the kitchen and helped Sophie start dinner while the men were showering.

John took ridiculously fast showers. She had no idea how he did it. But barely five minutes had passed when John reappeared, his hair still damp and wearing clean khaki shorts and a blue T-shirt. His eyes looked very blue in his tanned face as he wrapped his arms around her and nuzzled her neck.

Trying to ignore the ripples of pleasure at his embrace and his obvious affection, she sniffed and said, "You smell much better now."

He was about to reply when his phone rang. He pulled it out of his pocket, glanced at the screen, and then silenced it.

"Who was it?"

"Chuck."

She huffed. "You shouldn't ignore Chuck's calls. What if it's important?"

"I'm still on sabbatical for another two days."

"That doesn't mean he can't call you!"

He laughed softly and pressed a little kiss on her lips. "I'll call him back later."

Betsy knew this was a significant step for him—not jumping on a work call immediately, to the detriment of anything else in his life—and she was proud of him for it. So she wrapped her arms around his neck and kissed him enthusiastically.

"Excuse me," Mark said in a loud voice. "Coming through here. Not seeing anything. Just passing by."

Betsy was giggling as they broke apart, and she watched as Mark gave his brother a soft punch on the shoulder. "When you get a chance, I have something to tell you, something you're obviously too clueless to figure out for yourself."

This was enough to pique John's interest, and he followed his brother into the kitchen. He took Betsy's hand first though, pulling her along with him.

John was unabashedly excited about his brother's news. It would be his first niece or nephew, and he had a grand time making up a bunch of outlandish names to make up for the very traditional John and Mark their parents had named the brothers.

All four of them had a wonderful evening, making dinner, eating it, and then sitting around the table for a couple of hours afterward, talking well past dark.

Betsy supposed maybe other people had such evenings all the time, but she almost never had. She enjoyed it more than she would have expected.

She'd always believed that these kinds of experiences only happened to other women. But this was real. John's love for her was real. The future they were going to start together was real.

And tonight was real—eating and laughing with these people she loved.

It was one of those small miracles of life. Her mother had always called them blessings.

And no matter where else their lives would take them, she knew there would be more of them to come.

~

Seven months later, Betsy was asking, "Do we have to walk so far?"

John glanced over and saw she was slightly rosy from the sun, although the December afternoon was cool and brisk. Her expression as she asked the question was confused and slightly frustrated.

He tried to put on a casual demeanor, although his heart was already pounding from nerves and excitement and a kind of urgent vitality he'd almost forgotten he could experience earlier this year.

Betsy sighed and gazed out over the beach and the Atlantic Ocean, both of them gleaming in the sunshine of a perfectly clear winter day. "This looks like a good spot right here."

"I can still hear the cars on the road," he said with a kind of blithe matter-of-factness he hoped would be convincing. He reached out to take her hand as they walked farther south from where they'd parked. "And that guy fishing over there is annoying."

Betsy turned back to stare in astonishment at the completely innocent lone fisherman standing on the beach in the distance.

He almost choked on his laughter at the look on her face, but he managed to control his expression and made a guttural sound as he dragged her along. "Come on now. I don't like this spot."

She huffed and rolled her eyes at him, although she fell into step with him easily enough. "What's gotten into you today?"

"Nothing has gotten into me."

"Well, something has gotten into you. You've been weird all day. Did my mom say something to you?"

"What would she have said?"

"I don't know. But I wouldn't put it past her to put pressure on you or something." She was peering at his face now, and he knew he had to be very careful.

He was so focused on the task at hand that he had trouble following her implications. "Pressure about what?"

"Pressure about... about us." Her face twisted in a way that was both ironically amused and embarrassed. "She might want you to be moving faster—with the relationship stuff I mean. But she's really not trying to... I mean, she just wants the best for me, for us. Don't get upset by anything she might say or hint about."

He understood what she was saying now. And truth be told, for the past two days, as they'd been visiting Betsy's mother on the Outer Banks for the Christmas holiday, the woman had made more than a few hints about John not wasting any more time. It hadn't bothered him at all. He knew what mothers were like, even though his had died long before she'd had a chance to give him a kick in the pants over such things. "I'm not upset."

"You're acting upset."

"I am?"

"Yes. Or weird or something. Is there something I should know about?"

"No, no." He was walking quickly, and he knew Betsy was having to take extra steps in order to keep up with his longer stride. But she'd figure things out soon enough, and he wanted to be in place and ready before she did.

"John." Her voice was slightly sharp now, and she stopped in the sand. "I don't like you to keep things from me."

He stopped too and turned to face her. He reached out and cupped her cheek with one hand. "Sweetheart, I'm going to tell you everything you need to know. I promise."

His words or his expression must have convinced her because her face relaxed visibly. "Then why are you being so weird?"

"I'm not being weird. I just want to find a good spot for our picnic."

"I know, but we only have an hour or two before we have to meet up with Mom. We can't go on an all-day hike up the beach."

"I don't want to go on an all-day hike. Just over there." He gestured farther on.

She sighed and continued walking with him without argument, much to John's relief.

They'd almost gotten where he wanted to go when she pulled to a stop again. "Wait! We've gone too far."

"What do you mean?"

"This part of the beach isn't public. It belongs to Balm in Gilead."

"Oh." He blinked. "I didn't realize we were so close."

She nodded farther up the beach. "Look. There's the back of the building."

"Well, it doesn't matter. I like this spot right here."

"But it's a private beach?"

"Who cares?"

"Zeke will care when he catches us trespassing."

"I don't care about Zeke."

"He'll yell at me."

John chuckled softly. "Then I'll yell at him back."

She rolled her eyes. "You would too."

He took a step forward. "Of course I would. You don't think I'd yell at anyone who was mean to the woman I love."

Her dry expression transformed into something soft and fond. "You're being weird again."

"Great. I thought I was being romantic."

Her brows lowered. "You were?"

"Well, I dragged you all the way back to Balm in Gilead, where I first fell in love with you, didn't I?"

He could see the flickering of thoughts on her face, as she was trying to work things out. "You did?"

John's heart was beating wildly again. He'd planned a whole speech, but it didn't seem right now. It didn't seem natural.

It didn't seem like him and Betsy.

He said, "You know I did. I guess I was probably in love with you before then, but it wasn't until I came here that I realized it. This is where it happened for me, for us."

Her mouth trembled slightly, amusement or emotion or both at the same time. "I know that. I meant you dragged me here on purpose. I thought you just accidentally went too far."

"Oh." He cleared his throat. "That."

She crossed her arms in front of her chest, like she was hugging herself. "What's going on, John?"

"I wanted to come out here, *back* here. This is where I wanted to do this."

"Do what?"

He stuck his hand into his pocket, and Betsy gasped audibly.

"Seriously?" she breathed.

He frowned at her. "I haven't even gotten it out of my pocket yet."

She reached out to clutch at his shirt. "*Seriously?*"

Joy was bursting in waves from his heart, at the shock and excitement and happiness—the *answer*—he could see clearly on Betsy's face. But he couldn't seem to get the damned ring out since the box and his fist around it wouldn't easily slide out of the opening. "Let me get it out of my pocket," he grumbled.

She waited for a moment, her breathing fast and uneven as she kept clinging to his shirt. Then she whispered, "Well, hurry up and get it out."

He growled impatiently and yanked out his hand. "There."

Betsy made a wordless sound, like she couldn't restrain whatever was bubbling up inside her.

John opened the box and took out the ring—a diamond solitaire on a simple gold band. Then he had to pull his hand away when Betsy reached for it.

"Let me ask you first," he said.

She took a deep breath and dropped her hand. "Okay. Go to it."

He cleared his throat and met her eyes, and was momentarily speechless at the love and laughter and knowledge he saw there. Then he managed to say, "I was only half living when you first brought me here seven months ago. And I was trying to... I was trying to earn my way into God's favor. I had no idea of the blessings he'd already given me and so many more he was about to. And you're the greatest blessing I can imagine ever getting. I'd like to share the rest of my life with you and *live* all the way with you. If that's what you want too."

"It is." Betsy's mouth was wobbling and so was her voice. She was so overcome she was close to tears. "Of course it is."

"Then would you marry me, Betsy, and be my sweetheart for the rest of our lives?"

"Yes!" She threw her arms around his neck and kept repeating, "Yes, yes, yes."

It was exactly the answer he'd wanted, and it didn't matter if he didn't deserve it.

He was being given it anyway.

He'd slid the ring onto her finger and was kissing her quite passionately when a sound from the distance diverted them.

They broke apart and both looked over, and Betsy gasped, "It's Zeke! He's seen us!"

It was indeed Zeke in the distance, striding toward them. The man had some kind of radar where this place was concerned. He could always sense when someone was breaking the rules.

"I hope you don't expect me to run away from him," he said, wrapping his arm around Betsy and pulling her against him.

"That would be my first instinct," she said, sneaking a little look down at her ring.

John liked the look of it there too.

"We can just say hi," John suggested. "Maybe we could go see Cecily too, while we're over here."

Betsy was giggling and shaking her head. "Fine. But you're the one who's going to have to explain to Zeke why we were trespassing on private property."

"Fair enough."

Zeke recognized them as soon as he approached, but he wasn't at all impressed with the fact that they'd just gotten engaged. In fact, he just snarled at the news.

But he figured he and Betsy were happy enough for all three of them, and even Zeke's glowers couldn't bring them down.

ABOUT NOELLE ADAMS

Noelle handwrote her first romance novel in a spiral-bound notebook when she was twelve, and she hasn't stopped writing since. She has lived in eight different states and currently resides in Virginia, where she writes full time, reads any book she can get her hands on, and offers tribute to a very spoiled cocker spaniel.

She loves travel, art, history, and ice cream. After spending far too many years of her life in graduate school, she has decided to reorient her priorities and focus on writing contemporary romances. For more information, please check out her website: noelle-adams.com.

Books by Noelle Adams

Tea for Two Series
Falling for her Brother's Best Friend
Winning her Brother's Best Friend
Seducing her Brother's Best Friend

Balm in Gilead Series
Relinquish
Surrender
Retreat

Rothman Royals Series
A Princess Next Door
A Princess for a Bride
A Princess in Waiting

Christmas with a Prince

Preston's Mill Series (co-written with Samantha Chase)
Roommating
Speed Dating
Procreating

Eden Manor Series
One Week with her Rival
One Week with her (Ex) Stepbrother
One Week with her Husband
Christmas at Eden Manor

Beaufort Brides Series
Hired Bride
Substitute Bride
Accidental Bride

Heirs of Damon Series
Seducing the Enemy
Playing the Playboy
Engaging the Boss
Stripping the Billionaire

Willow Park Series
Married for Christmas
A Baby for Easter
A Family for Christmas
Reconciled for Easter
Home for Christmas

One Night Novellas

One Night with her Best Friend
One Night in the Ice Storm
One Night with her Bodyguard
One Night with her Boss
One Night with her Roommate
One Night with the Best Man

The Protectors Series (co-written with Samantha Chase)
Duty Bound
Honor Bound
Forever Bound
Home Bound

Standalones
A Negotiated Marriage
Listed
Bittersweet
Missing
Revival
Holiday Heat
Salvation
Excavated
Overexposed
Road Tripping
Chasing Jane
Late Fall
Fooling Around
Married by Contract
Trophy Wife
Bay Song

Made in the USA
Columbia, SC
04 October 2017